The Blue Rebozo

OTHER BOOKS BY
PAMELA HUMPHREY

NONFICTION

Researching Ramirez:
On the Trail of the Jesus Ramirez Family

The Blue Rebozo

A NOVELLA

PAMELA HUMPHREY

Phrey Press

www.phreypress.com

Revised Edition

ISBN-13: 978-0996877039

Dedicated to those who pass down their family stories.

Preface

Census records, old photos, and other documents only tell part of a story. When researching my great grandmother's family, I searched census records, marriage records, military records, birth records, and death records. To that research, I added stories that were passed down. The factual information gathered and stories passed down, along with photographs, are recorded in my first book, *Researching Ramirez: On the Trail of the Jesus Ramirez Family.* In my research, one ancestor stood out – Petra. The facts of Petra's life were interesting. Stories passed down about her were captivating. I often wondered what life must have been like for her.

In the book *In Search of the Chili Queen: On the Fringes of the Rebozo,* I read that a rebozo would sometimes be given as a means of proposal. A *rebozo* is a shawl or scarf, usually woven, that has fringe along opposite edges. It can be used as shade from the sun, protection from the cold, a way to carry infants, or simply for the beauty of the accessory.

The rebozo sparked my imagination, and an idea developed—a way to tell the story. When creating the story, I started with facts, dates, and family history. Using my imagination, I filled in the rest of the story.

About 1872, Jesus Ramirez packed up his family, left Mexico, and moved to Texas. Jesusa (his wife), Clara (his mother), and his children: Jesus, Petra, Josefa, Estefana, Ignacio, Austacio, and Plutarco, all journeyed to Texas in a covered-wagon. It is possible that his daughters, Porfiria and Manuela, and his father, Jose, also came with them as well as Francisco and Lucio Guajardo. By 1880, the family was living in Guadalupe County, Texas. Francisco and Lucio were living with Jesus and his family and working on the farm. The oldest son, Jesus, was a shoemaker. He was married and living in nearby Wilson County.

Many of the stories that were passed down to me, I incorporated into the story. If you are curious about what parts of the story were based on my research, see the Facts, Dates, and Family History section at the end of the book.

Here is Petra's story as I imagine it.

- Pam Humphrey

Prologue
April 1874

The setting sun cast shadows that danced as Francisco paced in front of the porch. He turned when the door opened and saw Clara silhouetted in the candlelight from inside the cabin. She closed the door and shuffled toward the rocking chair. He ran to help her, but she waved him off. "I am old, but I can still walk to my chair."

He sat down on the porch steps and leaned back against the post. Chirping crickets filled the silence with their evening melody. Francisco knew that Clara understood the real reason he was outside. She watched people carefully and heard what went unsaid. He hoped the others believed him when he'd told them, "I'm just going out to enjoy the evening."

"Sounds like a fiesta in there," he said as he nodded toward the door. Candlelight twinkled in the windows. Voices and laughter bubbled from inside and drowned out the song of the crickets.

"Yes, the family is very excited about tomorrow."

Francisco buried his face in his hands. "My heart aches at the thought of tomorrow's ceremony."

"Oh, Francisco, I wish I could tell you that all will be as you dreamed, but I don't know what the future holds. I am sorry for your pain. She is choosing what she thinks is best."

※

Inside the cabin, Petra smiled as her family talked about the upcoming nuptials. Her smile hid the trepidation that she felt. Tomorrow she would marry. She would become the wife of a man much older, a man she barely knew.

※

Clara got up from her chair and patted Francisco on the head. "Don't stay out too late."

Francisco nodded. "The hardest part is seeing how nervous she is. She is not marrying for love."

"You have been friends for many years, and you know her well," Clara said, turning to face him, "but you cannot know what is in her heart and thoughts."

Francisco sighed and walked to the door with Clara. As he stepped inside, Petra met his gaze. He smiled back at her.

"I hope you will be able to attend tomorrow," she said. "Can you manage a day away from the fields?"

"I will attend," he said, "And, Petra …"

"Yes?"

"I wish you much happiness."

The Blue Rebozo

Chapter 1
October 1879

Petra smiled as Alcario and Samuel ran circles around her, laughing. "Ay! Be careful, boys. Watch out for the water bucket."

She continued down the well-trodden path watching as the boys waded into the grass laughing and playing. In the distance sat five sharecropper cabins, all in a row. One of those cabins was home.

As they neared their cabin, Petra shaded her eyes against the sun and looked out across the field. She strained her eyes and tried to focus on the black specks in the distance. She glanced at her two boys, still running alongside her and then shifted little Candida who was wrapped to her back with a colorful rebozo. Looking up again, she could now make out two horses galloping toward the cabins.

"The men are back early. I did not expect them until much later," Petra said aloud, quickening her steps and planning what she could quickly prepare for a meal. The beans that she'd put on the stove would not yet be ready. There were some tortillas, a handful of eggs, and a few vegetables that she could combine for a quick meal.

As the horses drew near, fear gripped her, and all thoughts of food vanished. One rider was slumped over, his horse being led by the other rider. Running to the porch, she set down her bucket and released her toddler from the rebozo. Calling to her mother who lived in one of the nearby sharecropper cabins, she sat Candida on the porch, asked the boys to watch out for their sister, and told them all to stay near the porch. Petra pulled her skirt up to her ankles and began running toward the horses. The hem of her skirt snagged on twigs and thorns as she ran. Closing the distance between them, she saw that it was her husband that was slumped in his saddle. The other rider, her life-long friend, Francisco, called out to her, "Get the bed ready. Once we get him inside, I'll go for the doctor."

Petra rushed back to the cabin. Grabbing the bucket, she ran to the bedroom, yanked back the covers on the neatly made feather bed, and laid rags and linens within reach. Her thoughts tumbled over each other. *What happened? The children! I need to get the little ones off the porch.*

The sound of the horses snapped her back to reality. She ran back outside and saw her mother, Jesusa, holding Candida. The boys were standing beside their abuela (grandmother). The worry on Jesusa's face told Petra that she'd seen the man slumped over the horse. Francisco pulled up on the reins and stopped the horses in front of the cabin. He quickly jumped off his horse and caught the other rider as he slid out of his saddle. Petra helped Francisco move her husband into the bedroom and onto the bed.

"Dios Mio!" Petra gasped. "My God!"

Her husband's shirt was soaked with blood. He was unconscious and barely clinging to life. There was a gaping wound in his abdomen.

"He was stabbed by a stranger ... a stranger asked for a ride ... rode behind him on his horse for a little ways ... then he stabbed him." Francisco caught his breath between phrases. He started for the door. "I'll go get the doctor." He patted Petra on the shoulder then hurried out of the house.

Petra jumped into action. She tore open her husband's shirt and pressed folded linens against the wound. She stayed that way until the doctor arrived.

Her husband was strong but often described as thin and wiry. Now he seemed frail. The frailty she saw as he lay on the bed frightened her. She prayed that her husband would stay alive until he doctor arrived to mend his wound. "Please don't die, Mr. Torres. Please don't die."

He was twenty years her senior, and the habit of calling him Mr. Torres had not ended when they married five years ago. He chided her about her formality, but he was not chiding now. He lay almost motionless, barely breathing.

The sun was sinking toward the horizon when she heard the wagon. The doctor had finally arrived. He nodded a somber greeting as he walked over and examined the patient. Francisco followed him in and asked nervously, "Is he...?"

"Alive, but only barely," Petra said.

"I am going to the house to tell your family what happened. I'll be back soon," Francisco said.

"Thank you for bringing him home to me," she said, following him out. She stood on the porch and watched as he walked away. Looking down at her blood stained dress and hands, she was overwhelmed by worry and tried to calm herself with deep breaths. Her thoughts troubled her. *The wound was severe. Would the doctor be able to mend it?*

Afraid of what awaited her in the house, she delayed any bad news by lingering on the porch. She wiped her hands on her apron trying unsuccessfully to clean them. After a minute, she took a deep breath, gathered her courage, and walked back inside.

As she entered the bedroom, the doctor looked up and frowned. "There is nothing I can do for him. I am very sorry. He is alive, but I cannot repair the damage. I have stopped the bleeding as best I can, but now we can only wait." He kept his eyes on the patient.

She walked to the bed and clasped her husband's hand in hers. Tears filled her eyes.

"I will stay for a while," the doctor continued.

She nodded, but only stared into the face of her dying husband. Worry flooded her thoughts. *What would she do? How would they live without him?* Even though he was much older, she cared for him deeply. He was a good husband and father.

"Petra!" her mother called out as her parents entered the house.

"In here, Mamá," Petra said, wiping her tears.

"Francisco told us what happened. The doctor will be able to help, yes?" Jesusa hovered in the doorway. Petra's father, Jesus, stood behind her.

"There is nothing he can do. We just have to wait and see."

"Oh, Petra, I am so sorry. What can we do?"

"Please watch the children. I want to stay with Mr. Torres. Candida and the boys are still at your house?"

"Yes. The children are with your sisters. They will stay with us tonight. Your papá and I will stay here for a while. I will make you something to eat. Call to us if you need something."

Soon the smell of food filled the small house. Petra could hear her parents and Francisco in the kitchen as she stood near the bed holding the hand of her husband. Time slowed down. The waning light made it difficult to see, so the doctor lit a candle. He leaned down over the patient and then quietly patted Petra on the hand. "He's feverish. Infection has set in."

Petra listened carefully as the doctor gave instructions. He promised to return the next day.

Hearing the doctor getting ready to leave, Jesusa walked to the bedroom. "We are headed home, also. Send word if you need us. Food is on the stove."

Francisco told her that he would stay with Petra and help during the night. After the doctor and her parents left the cabin, he served Petra a plate of food. Grateful for the food, she sat and ate. He took over for her and mopped Mr. Torres' forehead with a wet rag. Empty and tired, he stared out the window until Petra's words pierced through the silence.

"Thank you, Francisco. Will you stay with him for a few minutes more?"

"Of course." Rewetting the rag, he laid it again on Mr. Torres. He heard the cabin door open and close and assumed that Petra was visiting the outhouse. Alone with Mr. Torres, he took the opportunity to talk to him.

"You cannot leave her. You are her family now. I was wrong to think that she did not love you," Francisco looked toward the door to be sure they were still alone. "When she married you, I was against it. But now I see the love for you in her eyes. And you are my friend. Please fight the fever, my friend."

Francisco stopped talking when he heard the door open. Petra washed her hands in the basin and then asked Francisco to dump it out the window. He did so, sat it back in place, and refilled it with water from the bucket.

"Go sleep, Francisco," Petra said, rewetting the rag.

"All right. Just call out if you need me."

In the next room, Francisco pulled off his boots, slid off his shirt, and lay down, his feet hanging off the edge of the bed. After tossing and turning, sleep finally found him as he lay sprawled on his stomach.

For two hours, Petra dabbed wet rags on Mr. Torres' forehead hoping that his fever would break, but it only worsened.

Francisco awoke when a screech owl screamed in the night. He wasn't sure how long he'd slept. He put on his shirt and walked back to Petra in his stocking feet. As he walked into the room, he stretched and said, "Petra, it is your turn to rest."

"I don't want to leave his side."

Francisco walked out of the room and returned carrying a chair. He sat it next to the bed.

"You can rest here by the bed, but you must rest."

"Thank you." Petra sat down and unlaced her boots. Sliding them off, she said, "Francisco, I am afraid he will not make it through this."

"Petra, please rest. You are weary. I will care for him while you rest." Francisco patted her on the shoulder.

"But you will wake me if …" Petra let the question dangle unfinished.

"Yes, I will."

Petra tried to sleep, but the feverish moans of Mr. Torres made it difficult. Finally she slept, and Francisco tended to Mr. Torres.

The night was cold. Francisco saw Petra shivering in her sleep, so he covered her with a blanket, pulled the shutters closed, and returned to his post. As he tended to Mr. Torres, the events of the day kept replaying in his head. The stranger had seemed a little crazy, but no one expected him to do what he did. Then Francisco remembered the look of fear in Petra's brown eyes when she saw Mr. Torres so badly injured. His heart ached at the thought. Over and over these thoughts played through his head leaving him exhausted. He was thankful when he heard the rooster announce daybreak.

The morning was gray and overcast. Petra awoke to the smell of breakfast cooking. Francisco smiled faintly, "Good Morning."

Laying the blanket on the foot of the bed, she returned his greeting, and checked on her husband. "He's getting worse."

Jesusa had come early and prepared breakfast. When she heard them talking, she carried in a plate of food for Petra and ordered Francisco to the table. "You need food and sleep." He didn't argue with her.

"Thank you, Francisco, for your help and for being here," Petra said.

Francisco nodded and walked out of the room.

Petra sat alone with her husband for a long while. She took his hand in hers. She could see that he was in pain. "If there is too much pain, Mr. Torres, you do not have to stay." She almost jumped when he faintly squeezed her hand. She gently squeezed his hand in return and repeated what she'd said. "If there is too much pain, you can go. You don't have to stay, Mr. Torres."

Minutes later, he was silent and motionless and no longer in pain. Petra sat silently, tears flowing freely, until the doctor arrived.

Jesusa greeted the doctor when he arrived. As soon as he walked into the bedroom, he saw that he was no longer needed. He offered Petra his condolences and walked back out to the kitchen. After Jesusa heard the news from the doctor, she thanked him for his efforts and walked him to the door.

An hour later, Francisco awoke and heard about Mr. Torres' death. Without delay, he walked over to Petra's cabin, and stood just outside the bedroom. His mind raced as he tried to think of comforting words.

"Have you slept?" Petra asked.

"A little. Sleep is difficult right now," he answered. Petra nodded her understanding. Francisco continued, "Petra, I do not even know what to say. Mr. Torres was a good man. I am sorry he is gone." Petra tried to reply, but no words came, only tears. "He needs a burial. I can make arrangements if you want. I will go and even dig the grave if necessary," added Francisco.

Petra walked over to Francisco and hugged him. "Yes, thank you."

She squeezed his hands briefly and walked back to the bed. Francisco walked out of the house, saddled a horse, and rode off to make arrangements for the burial of Mr. Torres.

The hours and days that followed were hard for Petra – the wake, the burial, and then trying to figure out how life would continue without a husband.

※

"You and the children will move back in with us," Jesus, announced firmly.

"But there is no room, Papá," Petra argued.

"There is always room for family," he said.

Petra packed up their belongings and moved back into her parents' sharecropper cabin. The house was already crowded. But now, her parents, her siblings, her grandmother, Francisco and Lucio, and she and her children would all reside in the two-bedroom cabin.

Chapter 2
November 1879

Francisco walked into the kitchen. Clara was the only one there. "Where is everyone?" he asked.

"Jesus and Jesusa rode over to visit with their son, Jesus." Dropping her voice to a whisper she added, "They are taking him the measurements so that he can make shoes for the children—their Christmas surprise."

Francisco looked around. "And Petra?"

"She walked down to the creek to get water."

"It hurts me to see her so sad. I relive that awful day in my head wishing I could change the outcome. She is too young to be a widow."

"Francisco, I told you before that we cannot know what the future holds, but also know that we cannot change the past."

"But, I wish there was something I could do to erase the hurt from her eyes," Francisco said as he ran his fingers through his dark, wavy hair.

"It will take time, but her burden of grief will lighten."

The front door opened and Alcario ran in yelling, "Help! She fell and now she cannot walk."

Francisco jumped up and was out the door in a flash. He could see Petra down the path leaning over someone on the ground. He hurried over and saw an embarrassed Josefa sitting down in the dirt.

"I turned my ankle. It will be fine," she said, but the tears in her eyes revealed her pain.

"Josefa, you are hurt. I saw you try to walk. You cannot," said Petra.

"I can carry you home," offered Francisco.

Seventeen year old Josefa blushed. "Thank you."

Francisco lifted her off the ground and carried her to the cabin. Petra followed close behind taking two steps for each one of Francisco's.

Clara stood waiting on the porch. "Bring her inside and sit her in a chair." As Francisco set her down, Clara pulled up another chair so that Josefa could elevate the injured ankle. Clara examined her ankle and then wrapped it tightly in strips of cloth.

Petra untied her rebozo and let Candida down. "The water! We left the buckets on the ground where Josefa fell. Abuelita, I will be back in a few minutes." Petra walked out the door, and Francisco was close behind.

When they arrived at the buckets, Francisco grabbed a bucket in each hand leaving only one for Petra to carry. He wished that he could carry the unseen burden that weighed so heavily on her.

"Thank you, Francisco," said Petra. "It seems that I say that often."

He smiled in response. Changing the subject, Francisco asked, "Is your brother making shoes for your little ones also?"

"Yes, I sent the foot tracings to my brother. They really need new shoes."

※

Josefa spent many hours that day in a chair with her injured foot perched on another chair. She dozed for a short while and awoke to a small bouquet of wildflowers on the table beside her. She smiled to herself and inhaled the sweet aroma of the bundle.

"Abuelita, who left these for me?"

"I do not know who left them,"

When dinner was ready, Petra helped Josefa to her chair. Francisco walked in just as they sat down at the table. During dinner, Josefa sat quietly trying to decide how and what she should say about the flowers. The others talked about the events of the day. When the conversation died down, Josefa looked at Francisco and said, "Thank you for the flowers." He looked puzzled for a moment, until Alcario answered, without looking up from his plate, "You are welcome, Tia Josefa. I'm sorry you were hurt. I thought flowers might help you feel better." Then he looked up and broad smile swept over his face.

Chapter 3
December 1879

Francisco lay in bed and listened as Petra cried outside on the porch. The sound of her grief was occasionally interrupted by Lucio's snoring. Since Francisco and Lucio slept in the sitting room, Francisco saw when she slipped out after everyone went to bed, and he heard her empty herself of her tears. But he didn't go out to comfort her. He knew that she needed the time alone. It was hard to lay there and listen as she cried, though. He felt almost an intruder in her grief.

The next morning started out cold and wet. But by the afternoon, the rains stopped, and the sun made an appearance. Petra asked Francisco if he would take her children for a short walk.

"Of course. I would be happy to," he said.

"Thank you. I want to wrap packages," she whispered.

Francisco winked and nodded. Then he called to the children. They donned their coats and then eagerly went outside.

He carried Candida. Alcario and Samuel walked alongside him. As they walked, they talked about the upcoming holiday.

"Tomorrow is Christmas Eve!" exclaimed little Samuel.

"Yes, and I am very excited about that," Francisco replied.

"They will make tamales tomorrow!" said Alcario.

"That is why I am excited," laughed Francisco.

"I hope we get an orange this year. I love oranges," said Samuel.

"Me, too," added Alcario.

The boys continued talking as they walked, but Francisco was lost in thought, contriving a plan.

When they returned, Petra gave a slight nod indicating that she had completed her secret task. The ladies were in the kitchen grinding corn for the masa. Jesus and his sons stood outside around the pit where the hog's head cooked. It would cook in the pit all night. In the morning the pork would be shredded and seasoned, the masa mixed with spices, and the tamales assembled and steamed. Everyone was looking forward to eating tamales.

The next morning Francisco rose before the others, saddled a horse, and rode into town. He hoped that by slipping out early, he would not be missed. In town, he walked into the general store just as it opened and looked around. The clerk nodded a greeting and asked, "May I help you find something?"

Francisco told him what he wanted, and the clerk walked over, picked up the last bag of oranges, and handed it to Francisco.

"On account?" asked the clerk.

"No," Francisco replied as he pulled money out of his pocket.

He settled up with the clerk, tied the bag to his saddle, and rode home. He slipped into the barn, hid his surprise, and then joined the others in the day's activities.

Seasoned pork simmered on the stove. The masa was mixed with spices and lard and then spooned into bowls. The ladies spread the masa on softened husks, added seasoned pork to the center, and then folded the husks with the masa and pork inside. The men kept husks soaking to soften them and replenished the ladies' supply often. The cabin smelled wonderful. Soon several dozen tamales were stacked in a pot on the stove, ready to be steamed.

The late afternoon meal of tamales, rice, and beans was a favorite treat—their traditional Christmas Eve meal—in the years when they could afford it.

The evening was festive, and everyone young and old, was excited about Christmas. That night, the stockings were hung, and the children, even the older ones, were sent to bed a little early. Petra and Jesusa put out gifts for the next morning—a new pair of shoes for each child. Into each stocking, they put an apple and a handful of pecans. Once everything was in its place, everyone went to bed. In the morning, after chores were completed, they would celebrate.

When the house was quiet and Lucio was asleep, Francisco slipped out to the barn and retrieved the prized oranges. He tied a note to the bag that read, "For Alcario, Samuel, and Candida. Share with your mamá." He climbed back into bed eager to see their faces the next morning.

He was so excited about the surprise that he did not see the figure quietly watching from the shadows. Petra stood silently until Francisco was back in bed, then she returned to her bed rather than going out to the porch. Tears wet her pillow. But tonight they were not tears of grief. They were tears of happiness and gratitude. Her heart was touched by the kindness of Francisco.

Chapter 4
January 1880

After half an hour of torrential rain, all that remained was a steady drip, drip of the lingering shower.

"Never have I seen so much rain! When will it stop?" Estefana complained.

"It is good for the land, but not for the little ones," Lucio chided. Lucio and Francisco were brothers that were from the same small village in Mexico.

Estefana understood the slight. "I am not little! I am thirteen."

"Estefana, go gather the eggs. It will give you something to do," said Jesusa, waving her hand as if shooing her out the door.

"Yes, Mamá," she replied as she tied on her bonnet and wrapped a shawl around her shoulders.

"I'll help," offered Lucio. He followed Estefana out the door. Laughter could be heard as they ran to the chicken coop in the rain.

Petra stood in the sitting room, peering through a small gap in the shutters. Three months ago, she'd lost her husband to the horrible act of a stranger. She'd moved in with her parents and often worried about the future. The weather these last few weeks mirrored her feelings. The skies were gray and overcast. It was the wettest month they had experienced in the seven years they'd lived in Texas.

The wooden shutters were pulled closed to keep out the rain, so the cabin seemed dark, even in the middle of the day. Petra's little boys were being entertained by their Tia Josefa while Candida napped. Alcario and Samuel covered their eyes, and Josefa hid a shoe in the sitting room. Then the boys scurried around and tried to find it. Their hunt was comical and entertained the grown-ups. The sound of laughter eased the stress of being confined indoors. Days passed slowly in the rain. Cows still needed to be milked, chickens still needed to be fed, but most of the field work waited until the rains stopped.

Petra's three brothers ran in and stood by the door dripping wet, leaving puddles all over the floor. Jesusa ordered the boys into the other room to dry off. "My house will never stay clean in this rain!" she said.

Francisco laughed. "Jesusa, your house is always clean."

Josefa wiped up the puddles, and Petra—who had moved to the kitchen—announced that food was ready.

Meal times were a favorite time for Jesusa. She loved being surrounded by her family. Even the rain could not dampen the joy of having so much family at her table.

※

Finally, in early February, the rains ended, and the sun was a more constant companion. Petra was glad to see the rains go away. Her children did not return home a muddy mess after running outside, and the house was less crowded because the family was not huddled indoors.

Petra finished feeding little Candida, looked out the window at her boys who were outside enjoying the sunshine, then sat down, and picked up her mending.

Clara, her abuelita, joined her in the sitting room and picked up her handwork. "Petra, it will not always be this way. You will marry again. Love will find you."

Petra remained focused on her mending. "Love? I think love is only in your stories, Abuelita."

"No, not only in my stories."

Just then the door swung open and Samuel, only three years old ran in yelling, "Mamá, Alcario fell."

Petra tossed aside her mending and rushed out the door. "What happened?"

"He was climbing the big tree!" Samuel answered, pointing to the large live oak that towered over them, obviously proud of his big brother.

Five year old Alcario lay on the ground. Petra knelt down over him calling his name. "Alcario! Wake up!"

His eyelids fluttered, and he opened his eyes. "Mamá, I made it to the top of the big tree! Well, almost to the top," he said trying to sit up, then moaned as the pain in his head became too much to ignore. "But I bumped my head when I fell."

Francisco heard the yelling and ran up from the barn, arriving moments after Petra. "The big tree? My! You are growing up," he said. Then he bent down and scooped up Alcario. He carried him inside and laid him on the bed. Petra sent her brother, Plutarco, to the stream to get more water. Ignacio saddled a horse and rode off to call the doctor. While waiting for the doctor, Petra sat with Alcario stroking his brown locks, telling him to lay still, and hoping the doctor would be there soon.

They didn't wait long for the doctor. After an examination, the doctor announced, "Bed rest should heal all wounds. He has a large bump on his head, but I think all will be okay."

Francisco added from the doorway, "It's a good thing you have a hard head, Alcario."

The doctor laughed, tousled Alcario's hair, and walked toward the door. "Send for me if anything changes."

Petra sat next to Alcario on the bed. "Please, please be careful, Mijo. I cannot lose you, too."

"Okay, Mamá." Alcario smiled up at her. "I wish you could have seen me. I climbed the big tree!" she could not help but smile.

He spent the next two days in bed. When his mamá was convinced that there was no permanent damage, she released him from the bedroom with a caution to stay out of the big tree at least for a few days.

Chapter 5
February 1880

Beads of sweat broke free of their clusters and trickled down Petra's face. She wiped them away with the back of her hand. She stood and stretched her sore and tired body. The February sun was high in the sky and pummeled her with its rays. It was unusually warm for an early spring day. The humidity was high causing the heat to stick to her skin.

The entire family, except Clara and Petra's little ones, were in the field planting cotton. The cotton harvest was their biggest source of income. As sharecroppers they planted, tended, and harvested the cotton. Once it was hauled to the gin and sold, they received a share of the money.

Thankfully the rains had stopped in time to plant. Bending down, Petra poked a hole in the dirt with a small stick, dropped in a seed, covered it with dirt, and then continued down the row.

Francisco glanced at Petra time and again as he planted his row of cotton seeds. He hoped that he could perhaps catch her eye, just to see her face. She'd lost her husband only four months ago. He thought that it was too soon to speak up about how he felt. "And, besides," he muttered, "what do I have to offer her but this hard-working life?" He did not like to see her so obviously sore from working in the field.

At dinner that night, Francisco and Lucio talked with Petra's father, Jesus, about how much they planted and what work awaited them tomorrow. It would be another full day in the field for the family. Sleep came easily to all that night. Petra lay down as soon as her kids were in bed.

She awoke to the smell of breakfast. Realizing that she'd overslept, she jumped out of bed, put on her calico dress, and pulled her hair into a knot. She smoothed the unruly curls back into place, and pulled on her boots. After lacing them, she hurried into the kitchen apologizing to her mother. "So sorry I overslept. Let me help." She poured cups of coffee and set plates on the table as the men came into the kitchen.

After breakfast, Estefana and Josefa cleared the table and cleaned up the kitchen. The rest of the family headed out to the fields. Petra wiped up little Candida's face and hands. Once everything and everyone was cleaned up, Estefana and Josefa tied on their bonnets and went out into the field. Petra handed Candida to Clara and kissed Samuel and Alcario atop their heads.

"Thank you for keeping an eye on them, Abuelita," she said. Clara nodded and smiled.

Petra hurried out the door to join the others. She put on her bonnet and tied up her apron. Filling her apron with seeds, she chose an unplanted row and started planting. Planting cotton was strenuous work, but it gave her time to think. Her thoughts turned to the future. There was no hope of moving out of her parents' house. It was not that she did not like living there, but she felt like a burden. When her lack of hope overwhelmed her, she redirected her thoughts to her children. Looking up, she saw the boys running and playing near the house. Clara sat in a rocking chair on the porch and Candida toddled around her. Petra smiled. But thoughts of her children brought thoughts of Mr. Torres. He would never see his children grow up. She tried to put all those thoughts out of her mind. Focused only on the task before her, she planted the cotton seeds. Caught up in the rhythm of the work, she sang quietly as she planted. When she realized that she was singing, she smiled to herself through misty tears. The ache would never be gone, but the sting was subsiding.

After dinner, the men gathered outside as was their custom. They discussed the cotton, recent events, and sometimes, politics. That night Petra heard them saying that now was the time to pray for the rain to return. The newly-planted seeds needed water to grow.

While the men talked outside, the ladies stayed inside and cleaned up after the meal and then worked on their mending or handwork. They worked quietly until Clara addressed Petra. "I heard that you sang as you worked in the field today. Your heart is lighter?"

"Yes, Abuelita. Much lighter."

Clara smiled.

"But who told you, Abuelita? I was not singing loudly. I did not think anyone heard me."

"Someone heard you, not just anyone." Clara said and winked at Petra. Further questions were thwarted by the men returning inside.

Later that night Petra pondered her abuelita's curious words. Before sleep overtook her, she prayed. "Dear Father, um, God, thank you for taking away the sting and making my heart lighter. I do not pray often, but I heard Francisco and Papá say that we should pray for rain. Please, God, send rain to water our seeds. Amen."

She slept soundly that night, so soundly that she did not hear the soft, gentle rain that fell during the night.

※

Days later, Petra was awakened before the sun crested the horizon. Jesusa shook her. "Wake up, Petra! Pack up the children and go to your brother's house. Clara and Estefana will go with you. Plutarco rode ahead to let them know you are coming. Francisco took ill during the night. Many in the community have come down with this sickness. It spreads very quickly, and some have not recovered. We do not want it to spread to the children."

Petra quickly gathered what they needed for travel and moved the children out to the porch. Jesus hitched up the horses and pulled the wagon in front.

After everything and everyone was loaded, Petra ran back inside. She stood in the doorway and waved to Francisco who was laying on the bed in the sitting room. "Be well, Francisco. I am sorry to leave you, but I must keep the children safe."

Francisco waved weakly and was then overtaken by a coughing fit. Petra hurried out the door and hugged her mamá on the porch. "Please take good care of him," she said, holding back tears.

"Yes, Mija. We all want him to be well."

Petra climbed up and took hold of the reins. Clara was seated next to her, and Estefana sat with the children.

They rode along with only the children talking for many miles. Finally, Clara spoke, "You cannot stay with him. The children need you. You are all they have left. If you got sick…"

"You are right, Abuelita, but I feel so guilty leaving him. I cannot imagine losing Francisco."

Clara patted her hand. "I know. He is a good friend to you."

They arrived in time for the midday meal. Petra's brother, Jesus, helped Clara down from the wagon and then unloaded their things.

The days passed slowly for Petra while she was at her brother's house. She worried and wondered about Francisco. Each night she prayed, "God, please make Francisco well. Life would not be the same without him." Day after day, as she helped around the house and watched over the children, she hoped that word would come that Francisco was well. More than a week after she she'd said goodbye to Francisco, Petra had a vivid dream. In the dream, she was standing in a field. The grass was very tall, so tall that she could only see over the top when stretching up on her tiptoes. She couldn't see anyone around her. Looking at the grass surrounding her, she chose a direction. Parting the grass like she was opening a curtain, she walked and walked but could not find her way out of the tall grass. Discouraged, she stopped and looked up to gauge her direction by the sun. She heard a voice call her name, "Petra!" She inched up on her tiptoes and looked around. She could not see anyone. "Is anyone there?" she asked. She heard the voice answer, "Not just anyone." Petra ran toward the sound of the voice shielding her face from the grass as it whipped by her. "Where are you?" she called out. She stopped, hoping to hear where the answer came from. "It is safe now. Come home to me, Petra," the voice answered back.

Petra awoke with a start. Her heart raced. "Francisco," she whispered. She closed her eyes, and sleep returned.

In the morning she pulled her abuelita aside and told her about her dream. "He must be well. Hopefully news will come soon," Clara said. Later that day Plutarco arrived. He told them that they could return because Francisco was well again. So the next morning they loaded the wagon, said goodbyes to Jesus and his family, and headed home.

When Petra pulled the wagon to a stop in front of the cabin, she hurriedly unloaded the children and helped Clara down from the wagon. In the cabin, when she saw Francisco, she ran to him and threw her arms around him. "Thank God! I am so glad you are well."

Startled by her sudden and uncharacteristic display of affection, he gave into impulse and pulled her close. He leaned down and whispered in her ear, "You came home."

Chapter 6
April 1880

The small farmhouse bubbled with noise as the family sat down to dinner. So many people in one house made for tight quarters, but during meals, no one seemed to notice. Jesusa and her daughters set bowls of food on the table and then settled in their chairs. Jesus sat at the end of the table and offered thanks to God for the meal.

Petra noticed this change in the dinner routine and wondered what prompted it. Later, she would ask her father about it. She wondered what prompted the change. They'd often attended mass when they lived in Mexico, but here in Texas they rarely attended. Churches where they'd be welcomed were far away. To see her father pray outside of church made her curious.

Food was passed; tortillas were filled. "Mamá, the calavacita is delicious." Petra said. Everyone heartily agreed.

"Abuelita prepared it." Jesusa responded.

Petra knew that her mother was thankful for Clara, her abuelita. With the crowded and busy house, the extra hands were helpful. Jesusa often spent days working in the field or tending to their garden. Having Clara prepare the meal saved her much work.

"I am glad you like it. This is how I made the squash when your papá was a boy." Clara nodded toward Jesus.

"I helped grind the chiles." Estefana added. As the youngest of the girls, she sometimes spoke up to be noticed.

"Using the molcajete can be hard work," Lucio teased.

At the end of the meal, Jesus rose from the table, kissed Jesusa on the top of her head and thanked the ladies for dinner. Then he wandered outside. His sons, Ignacio, Austacio, and Plutarco, followed him out. Francisco and Lucio thanked the ladies for dinner and walked outside to join the others. Francisco stopped to scoop up Alcario and Samuel on his way out the door.

While Jesusa and her daughters cleaned up after the meal. Clara sat in the sitting room with her mending. Little Candida toddled up to her great grandmother. Clara put down her mending and lifted Candida into her lap.

"Abuelita, will tell you a story—our story," Clara said.

Jesusa and Petra exchanged a smile. They had both heard the story many times before, but it was the kind of story that no one ever tired of hearing. All of them eagerly waited for Clara's telling of the story. But for several minutes, she sat looking out the window. Her eyes danced as she sat quietly smiling, reliving a memory and then slowly she began her story.

* * * * * * * * * * * * * *

A long time ago before you were born, or your mamá was born, or your abuela was born, even before I was born when our family still lived near the big hacienda at the edge of the mountains, there was a girl – Leonor. Leonor was beautiful. Her long, black hair swayed gracefully as she walked, and they say her eyes were so beautiful that you could see into her heart when you gazed into them. But in her village, El Potosi, there was no man for Leonor.

One day in late summer, Leonor noticed a young man loading a wagon. She did not recognize the young stranger and asked her friends about him.

"That's Esteban!" They replied smiling. "He is new in the village. He's very handsome!" It was clear that news of his arrival had spread rapidly through the small village.

Leonor watched Esteban as he loaded a wagon, but quickly looked away when he glanced at her. She wondered how she could find out more about this stranger. Carefully she asked questions in the village, not wanting to draw too much attention to her interest.

She learned that Esteban moved to El Potosi for work. He was from another hacienda far away. He was young, but old enough to take a wife. That was a matter of much speculation among the villagers. El Potosi was rather small. Single, eligible men were not in the village long before someone was trying to match them up and marry them off.

Esteban had not missed the curious eyes of Leonor. He smiled as he passed her, and nodded in greeting. He decided to ask a few questions about her of his friends. He had not seen her before. During dinner that evening, he asked a friend, "Who was the beautiful Indian girl in the village today? I have never seen her before."

"There are many girls in the village!" His friend answered, laughing. "But beautiful girls? You must mean Leonor. She is the most beautiful." His friend trailed off in laughter. Esteban smiled and agreed.

That night as he lay wrapped in his serape waiting for sleep, he thought about Leonor. He wanted to see her again. Weeks went by, but he did not see Leonor in the village. He had no time to seek her out. It was harvest time, which meant long days in the field and falling asleep almost before he finished eating.

In the weeks since seeing Esteban, Leonor stayed alert when she walked about the village hoping that she would see him. One evening as Leonor walked in the village, she heard rapid footsteps behind her.

"Good evening, Hermosa," said Esteban. He slowed to a walk as he came up beside her.

Startled, surprised, and delighted, Leonor determined not to let him see her excitement. She answered calmly, "Good evening. My name is Leonor."

"Hola, Leonor. My name is Esteban. May I walk with you?"

Leonor nodded her consent, and they walked and talked about the harvest and the cooler weather. Leonor's mother heard them as they approached the small adobe home and hurried outside. Esteban introduced himself and accepted when she invited him to stay for supper.

Leonor watched as Esteban ate and talked with her family around the table. When he glanced her way, she looked at her food or engaged her mother in conversation. But Esteban knew she was watching. He hoped that one day she would not look away.

After the meal, Esteban excused himself from the table and thanked them for a wonderful supper. He walked to the door, but before walking out he turned and asked Leonor's father, "May I come again?"

Leonor's father looked over to her as she was clearing things off the table. She nodded without looking up. If she had, she would have seen the smile that spread across Esteban's face. Her father answered, "You are welcome to come again, Esteban."

Esteban smiled and promised that he would.

That night Leonor wrapped herself in her well-worn rebozo and replayed the evening in her head as she tried to sleep. She thought about Esteban's thin angular face, not at all unpleasant. In her dreams, she could hear Esteban's greeting "Good evening, Hermosa."

The next day, Leonor went about her tasks singing, half-expecting to be surprised by footsteps or a greeting. When the ladies gathered to work the corn, Leonor was asked many questions. She kneaded the corn masa and answered the questions about Esteban simply. "He came for supper. He may come again."

Her answer was met with gales of laughter from the older ladies, and looks of jealously or contempt from some of the younger ladies. "So simple the words, but so deep the meaning," added one of the older women in the group.

After a long day of soaking corn, grinding corn, kneading the masa, and shaping tortillas, Leonor was ready to be home. When the last of her tortillas were ready, she said "good day" to the other ladies and walked back toward her house. Every sound drew her attention. She hoped to see her Esteban. Her Esteban? She chided herself. He was not her Esteban ... but maybe one day...

Weeks went by before Esteban was able to return to Leonor's house. He was taking on extra work and laboring long hours.

* * * * * * * * * * * * * * * *

The sound of the front door opening halted the story. In walked Petra's father holding a sleeping Samuel. Alcario followed behind him, yawning. Clara looked down at the child in her lap, "Petra, she's asleep," she said.

Petra gathered Candida into her arms and settled her in bed. Then she tucked Samuel and Alcario in for the night. Clara patted Petra as she walked passed, "I'll tell more of the story another night. This old lady needs her sleep."

Goodnights were exchanged and everyone went to bed. Petra closed her eyes and tried to sleep. Sleep was often slow to come since the death of her husband six months ago. She was glad for the three little ones that lay sleeping near her; often, the rhythm of their breathing lulled her to sleep. She always enjoyed when Abuelita told the story, but especially now. Now it reminded her of happy times and warm memories. And right now she needed to be reminded of happy times. Maybe in warm memories she would find hope for the future.

Her parents were gracious to let her live with them, but the house was so crowded. Three younger brothers and two younger sisters were still living at home; two friends lived there, and then of course, Abuelita was there. The two-bedroom cabin was full of people.

Several days passed before Clara continued her story. After dinner one evening, Candida crawled up into Clara's lap. "Story," she said.

Clara laughed. "Abuelita will tell you more of the story. When we stopped last time, Esteban was going to visit Leonor again," Clara said.

Candida clapped with delight, excited to hear more of the story.

* * * * * * * * * * * * * * *

Leonor was busy getting food ready when her father and brother arrived from the fields. She was standing outside, leaning over the fire, stirring the beans, and warming tortillas on the comal. When she entered the house to set the crock full of beans on the table, she almost dropped it. Esteban was sitting at the table. Her father and brother exchanged a look and laughed. Leonor recovered quickly, ran back outside, and returned with a stack of hot tortillas. Food was passed around. Everyone ate and talked. They all enjoyed the food, company, and conversation.

Like before, Leonor watched Esteban during the meal, but looked away when he looked at her and would not meet his gaze. After supper, he asked if she wanted to walk for a bit. He offered his arm and she gladly accepted. Conversation flowed easily for them. Esteban told her of his journey to El Potosi. He talked about his family. His father had worked all his life in the fields. His mother was famous in their hometown for her handwork and weaving. His sister had married well and moved away.

After a while, he said goodbye and promised that he would return for another visit soon.

Each day, Leonor thought of Esteban and hoped that he would be sitting with them at supper that night. And he did become a regular at their table. At least once a week, he had supper with the family and then walked with Leonor. Many suppers and many walks, yet Leonor still did not meet his gaze. She knew that her eyes would say too much.

Esteban liked to watch her move through the room as she helped her mother after dinner. He liked the way her thick, dark hair cascaded down her back almost dancing when she walked. Every time he visited, he hoped that night she would not look away. Sometimes they saw each other during the day in the village, but Leonor only gave Esteban a quick look and a smile.

One night when Esteban came for supper, he walked outside with her father after the meal while Leonor helped her mother clean up. She was very curious about the discussion happening outside. She hoped that it was about her. It was not long before they were back inside and Esteban asked if she wanted to take a walk. "It's cold tonight," he warned.

Leonor looked up, met his gaze, and smiled from across the room. "When I walk with you, I do not mind the cold."

A smile spread across Esteban's face. He was her Esteban. He knew that now. He offered his arm to Leonor, and they stepped out into the waning light. They'd walked only a short distance when Esteban stopped.

"Leonor, when I left my family, my mother gave me one thing, something very special." Esteban paused trying to choose his next words. "I have told you about my mother and how she had a talent for weaving and handwork. She made this for me long ago. It was to be for..." He cleared his throat and then continued, "I have carried this with me tonight because I want to offer it to you." He pulled a folded woven bundle out from under his serape and began to unfold a blue, delicately-woven rebozo. The fringe danced in the evening breeze. "I love you, Leonor. My mother made this for me to give to my bride. Will you accept it? Accept me?"

Leonor had never seen anything so beautiful. Tears streamed down her face as she nodded. She quickly took off the tattered rebozo that she was wearing and let Esteban wrap his exquisite gift around her shoulders.

"Yes, Esteban, I love you, too."

"I know, Hermosa. Your eyes told me so."

* * * * * * * * * * * * * * * *

"We'll stop there for tonight. I am getting tired," Clara said and waved off help from her granddaughter as she rose from her chair. "Petra, I'll tell you more of the story tomorrow."

After Clara left the room Petra realized that someone else had been listening to the story from just outside. Francisco smiled as he came through the door. "Your grandmother is telling the story again?"

"Yes. Candida loves to hear it, but she always falls asleep. Maybe one day she'll hear the entire story."

Petra had known Francisco as long as she could remember. He and his brother, Lucio, had travelled with her family up from Mexico years ago.

Francisco gathered the little ones and helped Petra get them settled into bed. Once they were settled, Petra wandered outside. Francisco joined her as she stood staring up at the blanket of stars. For a long while they stood silently. Francisco spoke first. "I like having the kids here. Everyone is glad you are all here. We are sorry for what happened, but we are glad you are here."

Petra dabbed at her eyes with the corner of her apron. "Thank you. Some days I feel such a burden and wonder what the future holds. You are a good friend, Francisco."

Francisco nodded and they resumed their silence. When Petra turned to go back into the house, she squeezed his hand and said, "Goodnight."

"Goodnight," he replied. He wanted to add one more word. To him she was hermosa – beautiful, but the time was not right. He had known Petra all her life, and loved her almost as long. He knew that when she married six years ago, it was not for love. The house was even more crowded then and when Mr. Torres offered marriage, even though he was much older, she accepted knowing that it made life easier for her parents with one less person to clothe and feed. It was not an unhappy marriage. Mr. Torres had treated her well, but it was not like the love in Clara's story. Francisco knew that love blossomed in its own time. He determined to have patience and wait until the time was right. He walked inside and crawled into bed. He was looking forward to hearing the next part of the story.

Chapter 7
May 1880

One morning, after weeks of watching her father pray before meals, Petra saw him sitting alone with a book open in front of him on the table. "Papá, what is that book?" she asked.

"A Bible," he said, "Reverend Robertson gave it to me. Have you met him?"

Petra shook her head.

"He is a Methodist minister who came and prayed for Francisco when he was very ill. He comes out to the fields to talk with us when he comes around these parts. He tells us about God and the Savior that died for our sins. Some days he shows me verses, explains the meaning, and teaches me to read them."

"Is he why you pray before dinner and not just in church now?" Petra asked.

"Somewhat. More because of what I have learned. We do not need a priest to talk to God. We can speak to him on our own, anytime–that is praying."

Their conversation was interrupted when Francisco walked through the door. "Have you heard the news? There was another Indian attack," he said as he sat down at the table with them.

"Another attack?" Petra asked as she stepped to the counter and poured Francisco a cup of coffee.

"Yes, about a day's walk west of here," Francisco replied.

Jesus shook his head. He hoped that these attacks would stop. They brought back unpleasant memories of attacks near his village when he lived in El Potosi. And the recent attacks were getting too close.

Petra sat down next to Francisco at the table. She hated to hear of these attacks. They concerned her. "Was anyone hurt?" she asked.

"Yes. A crazy story, too. A man was killed while his wife watched out a window. Knowing that she and her young children would be next, she ran out with her little ones. Then…"

Petra was leaning forward hanging onto every word of his story. "They got away?" she asked.

"Well, she ran to the creek but then drowned her children. She was trying to save them from the Indians."

"How is that saving them? That's awful! What happened to her?"

"As the Indians came toward her, she started hollering, loudly. It scared them off. Some folks said you could hear her hollering for miles. I'm not sure what happened to her after that."

Petra wiped away a tear. She could not let her mind linger too long on the horrific story. It was too awful to be real. "I hope I never hear that story again. It's heartbreaking."

Francisco was instantly sorry that he'd told her the story.

"You say it happened about a day's walk from here?" Jesus asked.

Francisco nodded.

"Papá, is that near my brother's place?" Petra asked.

"Could be. Probably not too far away. I wonder if they had any trouble there. Francisco would you ride over and check in on them?"

"Of course. I will leave right away."

As Francisco got up to leave, Petra laid a hand on his arm. "Francisco, may I go with you?"

Francisco looked to Jesus for approval. Jesus nodded. There was no thought of impropriety, Francisco was like family. "Yes, take the wagon," said Jesus.

Petra went to Josefa and asked if she would watch the children. "We should be back late tonight," Petra told her.

Josefa assured her that the children would be fine and asked Petra to convey her greetings to their brother, Jesus, and his family.

Shortly, Francisco and Petra were perched in the wagon and on their way to her brother's house. The first hour passed quietly. As they bumped along, Francisco glanced over at Petra and saw concern knitted in her brow. "I am sure everything is fine at your brother's place," he said.

"Yes. I am sure all is well, but it will be good to see them."

"What is it that concerns you?"

Petra sighed. "I have not been far away from Alcario, Samuel, and Candida before. It is only for the day, but I miss them."

"Your family will take good care of them." Francisco said hoping to lessen her concern.

"You are right, Francisco. It is silly to worry. But I do miss them." After a few quiet minutes, she said, "Remember the journey from Mexico? Being in the wagon today reminded me of that trip."

"Yes. It seems so long ago now. My feet were sore and tired after walking so many days. It was a long journey."

For the next couple of hours they reminisced about life in Mexico, the journey to Texas, and the tumultuous first year in Texas.

"Losing your abuelito, Jose, was very hard. We were only here a few weeks before he passed. The journey was too much for him maybe."

"Yes, then losing my sisters was so much hard on Mamá. Porfiria and Manuela succumbed so quickly to their illness. Mamá's heart was broken. It was hard on the whole family."

Another half-hour passed in silence. Francisco wondered if maybe it was the right time to pour out his heart. He thought of Esteban, Leonor, and the rebozo. Francisco had nothing to offer Petra except himself. He glanced over at Petra and cleared his throat.

When she turned to look at him, he saw tears in her eyes. She wiped her eyes and explained before he could ask. "All the talk of memories. I was thinking of the day Mr. Torres died." She shook her head trying to erase the grizzly picture from her mind.

Francisco reached over and patted Petra's hand. Now was not the time. He listened quietly as Petra shared memories of Mr. Torres. Happy memories replaced the image of her wounded husband at the end of his life. She reached out and clutched Francisco's right hand. He turned and met her gaze.

"Francisco, thank you for your friendship."

He nodded, but would not allow himself to speak. If he opened his mouth, he would say too much. He gently pulled his hand from hers and moved the reins to his right hand.

When they arrived at her brother's house. Jesus and Urbana were surprised and delighted to see them.

"We were just about to eat," said Urbana. "Please join us."

After lunch, Francisco and Jesus went to his cobbler workshop—a small building behind the house. They spoke about the recent attacks. Jesus had heard about the nearby attack, but they had no trouble in their immediate area. Residents in the area were on edge, and travel at night was discouraged. It was too dangerous.

Petra and Urbana avoided talking about the attacks and instead talked about family news. Petra held her tiny niece—who was named after the Leonor in Abuelita's story—and watched her nephews play.

When Francisco walked back inside, Petra asked, "Should we go now?"

He exchanged a look with Jesus. "No, it would be dark before we arrived home. It would not be safe to travel after dark." He did not like keeping Petra away from her children, but he would never knowingly put her in danger.

When it was time for bed, Urbana laid out a pallet and blanket for Petra and handed Francisco a blanket. Their one-bedroom house was quite small and had little room for guests, so he was going to spend the night in the barn.

"See you in the morning. We will leave very early," said Francisco.

Petra nodded. He closed the door and walked to the barn. Flopping down onto the hay, he smiled as he thought of the uninterrupted hours he would spend with Petra on the way home. Sleep found him quickly, despite his smelly surroundings.

Petra lay awake thinking about her day and praying for her children. "… And please keep Francisco safe in the barn. Amen," she added at the end of her prayer.

※

Petra smiled as the cabins came into view. Francisco worked the reins and soon the horses were trotting toward the cabins. He laughed when he saw Alcario and Samuel running toward the wagon.

"You were missed!" Francisco said.

He slowed the wagon to a stop so that Petra could climb down. She ran to meet her boys. After hugs and kisses, they walked home hand in hand.

Once they were all back at the cabin—after hugs and greetings were exchanged—Francisco took Jesus aside and passed along all that he'd learned about the attacks. Stories of Indian attacks continued over the next few weeks, but none compared to the story of the woman hollering by the creek.

Chapter 8
July 1880

The morning sky looked ominous. Thunder rumbled, and lightning streaked across the sky. After a loud thunder clap, the clouds opened up and unleashed torrents of rain. A summer storm had rolled in and changed the plan for the day. Petra's brothers, Ignacio, Austacio, and Plutarco ran to the barn despite the downpour. Even in the rain, chores still needed to be done. Lucio hurried out to ensure their few chickens were in the coop and to gather whatever eggs had been laid.

Jesus looked out the door and shook his head. "Francisco, we will not be working in the fields today. This storm is not moving fast." He walked back and sat at the table, where Francisco sat sipping his coffee. Jesusa poured Jesus another cup.

Estefana sat on the floor playing with her niece and nephews. Having everyone inside during the stormy day would make for a long one. Clara saw that the family needed a distraction. The dreariness of the day could be seen in their faces. She announced that it was a good time to tell more of the story. Her announcement was welcomed. Jesusa and Josefa sat down and picked up their handwork. Petra quieted the children and then stood by the window looking out at the storm. Francisco and Jesus listened from the table.

Clara asked, "Where did I leave off?"

"Love," Francisco answered from the table, "Esteban announced his love."

"Ah, yes. Esteban gave her the rebozo and declared his love. I will start there."

* * * * * * * * * * * * * * * *

Leonor's eyes were windows to her heart, and when she gazed at Esteban, he saw how she felt. He knew she loved him. Esteban tenderly held her face in his hand and tilted her head so that she gazed into his eyes.

"Leonor, I only wish that you could see my love for you the way that I see yours for me. I am yours always." He leaned down and brushed his lips against her cheek. "I will begin building our own place in the village right away."

Leonor slid her hands around Esteban and buried her face in the curve of his neck. Looking up again, she whispered "Hurry, my love. I want to be with you, to be near you, to hear your heart beat when you sleep, and to feel you close to me when I wake."

Esteban drew her close, whispered "Hermosa," and gently kissed her.

That night, Esteban's dreams were full of love and plans for the future. The next morning, he awoke very early and began gathering materials to build a home, and then started his day of work for the hacienda. When his work was finished he discovered that men from the village had already cleared a spot for building, and work on the house had started. For weeks, he spent his days laboring in the fields for the hacienda and his evenings building the house. Others in the village were quick to help and eager to see the house finished. Soon, it started to look like a home.

Late one night as he finished the last of the house, he decided to meet with the priest the next morning. He rose early, ran to the chapel, and met with the priest. Arrangements were made for the wedding. When he finished at the chapel, he hurried to Leonor's house before heading out to the fields and found her in the garden. "Thursday," he said. "We marry on Thursday." Quickly he kissed her and sprinted off to the fields. "I'll be by tonight!" he called as he ran off.

Leonor stood there for several minutes after Esteban had gone. Thursday. In just a few days they would be married. She ran off to find her mamá and tell her the news.

That evening after supper, Leonor's father patted Esteban on the back. "Thursday you will marry. Good news calls for a celebration!" He pulled out his gourd rattles and began to play a rhythm. Leonor began to dance and the family cheered. Esteban joined Leonor in her dance which spurred more laughter and cheers. The evening continued like that for a long while until finally it was time for sleep.

"Goodnight, Hermosa," Esteban called as he walked out into the night. "Only a few more days!"

"A few more nights!" Leonor answered, laughing.

If happiness brings peaceful sleep, they both slept in perfect peace. Leonor awoke early to enjoy the stillness of the morning before she started her daily chores. She was delighted to see Esteban up early also. "The house is done." he said.

Together they walked and talked of the future. Leonor stopped and looked at Esteban. "What do my eyes say now?" Esteban smiled as he looked deeply into her eyes and answered her question correctly with a long and passionate kiss.

The next few mornings were the same. They walked in the quiet hours of the morning and talked of their life together. That was the only time they were alone together that week. Preparations for the wedding filled the time not spent working. Leonor, her mamá, and sisters prepared the food for the reception. Her father arranged for musicians. By Wednesday evening, everything was ready for the morning.

Thursday morning...

* * * * * * * * * * * * * * * *

Thunder shook the house. Lucio, Austacio, Plutarco, and Ignacio ran in dripping wet. "It is coming down in buckets," Lucio said.

Josefa quickly ran to grab something for them to dry themselves. While the boys went off to change into dry clothes, the ladies warmed them food and coffee. Francisco relinquished his seat at the table, moved to the sitting room, and watched the rain out the window. Once things settled down, Clara began again.

✶ ✶ ✶ ✶ ✶ ✶ ✶ ✶ ✶ ✶ ✶ ✶ ✶ ✶ ✶ ✶

Esteban had arranged for an early wedding. He did not want to wait all day to marry his beautiful Leonor. Leonor awoke early, helped her mamá with a few last minute preparations and then went to get ready. She washed her hands and face and put on a white, cotton dress. Leonor's deep caramel skin and dark hair stood out strikingly against the white of her cotton dress. Her Mamá braided ribbons into hair. Then she picked up the blue rebozo and draped it delicately over her head. It cascaded down her back and over her arms.

Her father smiled broadly when Leonor walked into the kitchen. "As beautiful as your mother. Esteban is a lucky man."

Once everyone was ready, Leonor stepped out of the house and was greeted with cheers by friends and family. Her father offered her his arm and offered his other arm to her mother.

Esteban could hear the procession coming toward the chapel. Standing outside the chapel as guests took their seats, Esteban drank in the day. The February morning was cool but not cold, and there was snow still resting on the mountaintops.

Esteban stepped into the chapel, took his place at the front and waited. Leonor would arrive soon. The chapel was long and narrow. Dark wooden support beams stood out in contrast to the white-washed adobe walls. A small railing near the front separated the pews from the altar.

Once the crowd was seated and hushed, the Padre began the ceremony. On cue, witnesses walked down the aisle to their appointed spots and then everyone stood to their feet as Leonor and her father walked down the aisle. Leonor was beautiful! Esteban beamed at the sight of her in the white cotton dress and blue rebozo, barefoot, with ribbons braided into her hair. He could not take his eyes off of her. At the front, Leonor took Esteban's hand.

Leonor smiled at the sight of Esteban in his new white shirt. She could barely focus on the words of the Padre. The ceremony continued in the traditional way. The Padre indicated when it was time for them to kneel. They knelt at the altar and the lasso was placed over them. She echoed the vows and accepted the coins offered by Esteban. At the very end, Esteban sweetly kissed his bride.

Now it was time for the parade! The happy couple exited the chapel to the sounds of cheers, applause, and bells. Forever Leonor would remember the sound of the bells ringing in the bell tower on that day.

A few friends hurried off to set up for the fiesta. Leonor and her mother had prepared many dishes as had other close friends. A good fiesta needed lots of food and music!

Musicians played and sang as the crowd walked through the town. Neighbors leaned out of windows shouting well wishes. The parade made its way through the town to the plaza where they celebrated the joyous event. Ceremony, music, laughter, and feasting filled the morning and afternoon. Esteban was always near his bride. Her eyes told the depth of her joy.

Many weeks of hard work had gone into building the small adobe house. That day it became their home. Amidst cheers and shouts, they entered the house. Esteban, with the help of his mother-in-law, had stored up some food in the house. No one expected them to leave the house for several days. That night, they were happy to be alone together.

Just as the sun peered over the horizon, Esteban awoke. Famished, he grabbed a tortilla and stood quietly looking out the small window. Occasionally he turned to look at Leonor as she slept. She was wrapped in the blue rebozo. Never before had the rebozo seemed more beautiful. He wondered how his heart could contain so much happiness.

Leonor slowly opened her eyes and lay there studying Esteban as he looked out the window. She loved everything about him: his dark, sunbaked skin, the mop of brown hair on his head, and his hands; she loved his hands.

For days they did not leave the house, delighted with their time together. But eventually, they did emerge and married life began. Esteban continued his work in the *fields and worked hard to provide for his bride. He hoped that children would soon be added to their home.*

* * * * * * * * * * * * * * * * *

"Speaking of children, Abuelita, I should get mine something to eat." Petra said as she walked to the kitchen. Everyone agreed that food was a good idea. The storytelling would have to wait until later.

After lunch, Petra saw that the clouds were beginning to break apart and blue sky was peeking through. She pulled her sister aside. "Estefana, do you mind watching my little ones? I want to go to town now that the weather has cleared."

"Not at all," Estefana replied.

"Mamá, I am going to walk to town now that the storm has passed. Do you need anything from town?" Petra asked her Mamá.

"No, I do not need anything from town. But please be careful," Jesusa replied.

"Jesusa, would you like me to take her into town in the wagon?" Francisco offered.

"Ay, yes, Francisco. What a good idea! So much better than walking on muddy roads."

Francisco climbed into the wagon and offered a hand to Petra. She gathered the layers of her skirt in one hand and grabbed Francisco's hand with her other. Then she pulled herself into the wagon, sat down, and smoothed out her skirt. Francisco took up the reins and coaxed the horses into motion.

They rode along quietly for a while. Petra occasionally commented on a neighbor or the passing storm. Francisco was preoccupied with his thoughts, composing what he would say to Petra if he allowed himself to unleash his tongue. Two months ago when they were alone together on the way to her brother's place, he wanted to tell her of his love, but it was not the right time. Was now the right time? he wondered.

He opened his mouth and all at once, all the things that he been hoping to tell her poured out, but not in the way he wanted to say it.

"Since I was 5, love, and the children. Could you be my Hermosa, I mean, Beautiful Petra, for a long time and marry me."

Petra stared at him, speechless. Francisco shook his head and started over.

"Petra, I have loved you for a long time. I love you and the children. To me you are hermosa, beautiful. I want to marry you."

With all his thinking and declaring, Francisco failed to notice the building clouds and second line of storms moving over the area. Petra did not have time to respond before the sky opened up and rain poured down. Thunder rumbled, and lightning splintered across the sky. Francisco saw a barn in the distance and steered the wagon in that direction. Moments later he pulled the wagon into the barn, jumped down, and closed the doors. He lifted Petra out of the wagon, and they climbed up into the hay loft, away from the animals.

Francisco lay back on the hay, hands tucked behind his head, and glanced sheepishly at Petra. "You think I'm crazy?"

Petra looked at Francisco and saw his tall muscular frame, dark wavy hair, and soft brown eyes. Feelings she'd never contemplated bubbled in her heart. She responded to his questions by sliding up next to him, cupping her hand against his clean-shaven cheek, and kissing him. For the first time, her heart knew the kind of love described in Abuelita's stories. She now understood how Leonor felt when she looked at Esteban. Petra leaned down and kissed Francisco again; he responded by wrapping his arms around her and pulling her close. While the storm raged outside, Petra gave herself to Francisco.

※

"Abuelita, will you tell us more of the story while we wait for the storm to pass?" Estefana asked.

"Not now. Petra is not here. I want Petra to hear the story," Clara replied.

Jesusa was concerned. "They are caught in this. I am so glad Francisco was with her. He will keep her safe."

"Yes, Jesusa, Francisco will bring her home safely. Do not fret," Jesus said as he drew her close and kissed the top of her head.

"I know I should not worry. But it has been raining for more than an hour." Jesusa stood staring out the window twisting her apron and willing the storms to pass.

※

Once the storm passed, Petra's pragmatism quickly returned. "We must go home. Mamá will be worried. I can go into town another day."

"Maybe we can take the wagon," added Francisco with a wink as he lifted her into the wagon.

Petra blushed, smoothed her skirts, and picked the hay out of her hair. She slid close to Francisco and looped her arm through his. "Ask my father. If he gives his blessing, I will marry you."

Francisco whistled all the way home.

※

Once the rain stopped, Jesusa kept looking toward the door hoping Petra and Francisco would return. Soon she heard footsteps on the porch. The door opened and in walked Petra with Francisco close behind.

Francisco recounted how they had gotten caught in the storm and taken shelter in a barn, but he conveniently left out certain parts of the story.

"We never made it into town. We did not want anyone to worry," Petra added.

Clara eyed them carefully as they talked, and when they finished telling their story she said, "I am so glad you found safety during the storm. Petra it is good that you were not alone. Will you come help this old lady make some dinner?"

"Yes, Abuelita," Petra replied. She stopped to kiss her children as she walked through the room. Clara chopped potatoes and a small bit of smoked meat. Then she simmered them in a pan with spices. Petra set the table and warmed tortillas. While they worked, Clara talked about life in El Potosi. She'd lived in the village almost 60 years. It was hard to believe that she left her home 20 years ago.

"We did not eat potatoes then; we had never heard of potatoes. Only rarely did we eat meat, but tortillas, we ate corn tortillas every day." Clara continued to reminisce until everything was ready.

"Dinner," Petra announced, and everyone gathered at the table.

As Petra turned to put the food on the table, Clara brushed something off her the back of her dress. "Hay. From the barn, probably." Petra hoped that no one else saw her blush. She knew that Clara had not missed it.

After dinner, Clara continued with her story.

* * * * * * * * * * * * * * * *

Leonor and Esteban loved each other. One night only months after the wedding as Leonor and Esteban lay beside each other, she took his hand and slid it over her stomach. "A baby," she whispered, "We are going to have a family."

Esteban and Leonor were very happy. Dionicio was born before they had been married a year. Esteban beamed with pride as he told everyone that Leonor had given him a son.

Two years later Josefa was born. She was a beautiful baby, very much like her mother. When Josefa was two, Leonor and Esteban had another baby girl. They named her Clara.

* * * * * * * * * * * * * * * *

"Abuelita, that's you!" Estefana interrupted gleefully.

"Yes. That was me," said Clara. "I don't think I will tell the story tonight. The rainy day made me tired." Clara rose from her chair, kissed the children, said goodnight, and went to bed.

After Petra put the children to bed and said goodnight to her parents, she walked out to the porch. The day was ending so differently than it began. When she woke this morning the sky was filled with dark clouds and things looked ominous. Now the sky was clear and she could see thousands of stars. The stars twinkled a chorus that echoed the joy in her heart. She turned as she heard the door open and wiped a tear.

Francisco walked up behind her and slid his arms around her waist. "Why the tears?" he asked.

"I am happy."

"So you cry?" Francisco asked, laughing.

Petra laughed also. "Francisco, I had no idea you felt this way. Why did you never say anything?"

"I was only seventeen when you announced your marriage to Mr. Torres. I could not afford to marry, so it seemed a bad time to say anything. When he died, my heart ached to see your pain, but after a while, I had hope again. I waited because I knew you needed time to grieve."

"Oh, Francisco! I didn't know you'd loved me so long," Petra said. "So why today?" she asked.

"I did not plan to. I wanted to, but I thought I needed to wait longer. But your abuelita's story has me thinking of you all the time. Today, my heart just came pouring out."

Francisco stood almost a foot taller than Petra. She felt at home in his arms. She leaned her head back against his chest, and breathed in the moment.

"Francisco, you were right not to tell me before, but I am very thankful for the powerful storm that caught us by surprise today."

Francisco leaned down and kissed her on the cheek. "I will talk to your father tomorrow."

Petra quietly made her way to bed trying not to wake Estefana, Josefa, Clara, or her children, who all shared the room with her. It sounded as if they were asleep.

She almost jumped when Abuelita whispered, "He's loved you a long time. Now you see that love is not just in my stories."

"Yes, Abuelita. Now I know the love that Leonor felt for Esteban."

"Goodnight, Petra. Sweet dreams," Clara said as she pulled up her covers.

The next day, when Francisco and Jesus were alone working in the fields, Francisco took the opportunity to talk with him.

"Jesus, you know I am grateful that you brought me to Texas and that you treat me as a son."

Jesus nodded.

Francisco cut straight to the point. He knew that Jesus was not one for small talk. "I love Petra. I want to marry her. Will you give us your blessing?"

Jesus nodded again, never taking his eyes off his work. "Only wait until October to marry. For her sake, wait until she's been a widow a year."

Francisco agreed and thanked Jesus. They returned to their work in silence. The rest of the day, Francisco anticipated telling Petra the good news and wondered how he and Petra would present the news to the family. How long should they wait to announce it? Francisco's questions were all made moot when he sat down to dinner.

After saying the prayer Jesus announced, "Francisco asked to marry Petra. I gave my blessing. If Petra agrees, they will marry in October."

Clara smiled knowingly. The rest of the family sat stunned while Jesus began to eat. They looked to Petra for her answer. She nodded, smiling at Francisco. Then, all at once, the questions started.

"Petra, how long? I did not know." Jesusa asked

"Yesterday, Mamá, we talked when we were headed to town," Petra said as Francisco nudged her under the table.

In a short time, all the other questions were answered and congratulations were given. After the meal, they all sat down and Francisco asked if Clara would continue the story.

"Yes, Francisco, for you, I will continue the story." Clara answered with a gleam in her eye.

* * * * * * * * * * * * * * *

Esteban and Leonor were happy. Their family was growing, and there was plenty to eat. Life was good. But one day grief and sadness visited their growing family. Shortly before my younger brother, Hemeterio, was born, Josefa became ill. None of the herbs or other remedies cured her and their little girl slipped into the hands of God.

Leonor mourned her daughter deeply, and it hurt Esteban to look into Leonor's eyes. Hers was a pain that he could not heal. Many nights he held her close as she cried into his shoulder. What she needed most was to have him by her side. Slowly her heart healed and although she never forgot, the pain in her eyes was replaced by happiness once again.

After Hemeterio, they had Jose Maria, and then Jacinta, followed by Lucas, Santos, Manuel, and Bruno. Imagine a house with so many boys!

During this time as their family grew, so did the village. It still was not large, but more adobe houses were being built as people moved down out of the mountains or in from other areas to work at the hacienda.

When I was about twelve years old, stories of fighting and war drifted into the village. At first it all seemed far away, but at times the fighting was closer and we worried that it would affect life in the village. For years it went on outside the village, but life in the village stayed the same.

When I was nineteen, I fell in love. Jose and I both grew up in our small village. His father had died when he was young, and Jose worked hard to take care of his mother. The story of our love started one day when he passed me in the village, but instead of a quick greeting or a simple nod, he stopped and asked about my day and my parents.

This happened over and over during that week. One evening when I was talking to my mamá while we did our chores, I told her about the encounters. She suggested that I invite Jose to dinner.

So the next time he saw me and stopped to make conversation, I waited until he seemed to have exhausted his questions and then asked if he wanted to come to dinner. He accepted and then, well... then we married.

* * * * * * * * * * * * * * * *

"Abuelita, you are skipping parts of the story," Estefana interjected.

"So I am. I will tell the whole story … tomorrow."

The children were put to bed, goodnights were said, and the house soon became quiet. Petra lay still for a long time before sliding out of bed and walking out to the porch. Moments later the door opened and Francisco was by her side.

"I am sorry I did not get to tell you first. I did not expect him to announce it. I thought that tonight I would tell you quietly," he said apologetically.

"I am very happy he said yes. The hard part will be waiting, but I understand why," Petra responded. She leaned her head on his shoulder and enjoyed the closeness.

※

The following night, Clara resumed the story filling in the parts that she skipped.

* * * * * * * * * * * * * * * *

Jose came for dinner and we had a very nice evening. A week later, when he stopped to ask about my family, I invited him to dinner again, and he gladly accepted. On that visit, my father told him that he was welcome anytime. Esteban, my father, knew what it was like to be a young man in love.

After that Jose was visiting two or three nights a week. One evening he sat and talked with my father after dinner. I heard most of the conversation. Once the terms were settled, my Jose walked across the room and right there asked me if I would marry him. Of course I said yes. He kissed me quickly and told me he would make arrangements for the wedding. So soon after, we were married. I remember that day well.

It was July. I wore the dress that my mamá had made, and she braided my hair. Once I was dressed, she walked to the corner of the room and pulled out her blue rebozo.

My mamá, Leonor, walked up to me, draped it over my head and said, "Clara, this belongs to you now."

It was so precious to her. She wore it only on special occasions, but instead of wearing it on my wedding day she gave it to me.

At the chapel, Jose was waiting for me by the altar. I remember how handsome he looked and how he smiled when he saw me. So many good memories.

I was wearing the blue rebozo when I walked with Jose one evening after we had been married only a couple of months. We were holding hands as we walked. That was the night I told him that our family was growing. Jose was so excited.

In May, Jesus was born. He spent many months tied to my back in that blue rebozo. Always careful not to let it *get too tattered or too worn, I finally put it away, and used a different one for the everyday.*

Little Jesus had just started walking when the news of an independent Mexico reached the village. Our families had been in Mexico long before the Spanish arrived, and their arrival had changed the way of life for many tribes. But the news of an independent Mexico did not change the village much, only that the priest no longer labeled us "indio" or "mestizo" at baptisms and weddings.

Our family continued to grow. After Jesus, we had Casildo, then Paula, and Juliana, then Valentin, and Felipe, and Nicolasa, and Lucia, and Gabriela, then Agapita. We were so happy, but the years go by so fast. It seemed that one day I was holding Jesus, the next day he followed his dad into the field to work, and the next he was telling us that he wanted to marry.

* * * * * * * * * * * * * * * *

"The next part is best told by one who holds the memory closest." Clara turned to look at Jesusa. "Will you tell the next part of the story, Jesusa?"

Jesusa nodded. "Yes, but not tonight."

That night as Jesusa readied for bed, she slid a box out from under the bed and opened it. Jesus walked up behind her and kissed her on the neck as he put his arms around her and looked over her shoulder.

"You still have it," he said quietly.

"Yes. It holds so many memories," Jesusa replied. A single tear slipped down her cheek as she fingered the woven blue threads.

After she returned the box to its place, Jesus turned her to face him and said, "Jesusa, I keep my memories in my heart. And my heart is always and forever yours. The blue rebozo is beautiful, but I love the one that wore it." Jesus kissed her, and they lay down for the night, remembering how it felt to be young.

Chapter 9
August 1880

Weeks went by before Jesusa continued the story. One night the family gathered in the sitting room after dinner, and Jesusa started telling the story where Clara left off. Jesus stood on the other side of the room leaning against the wall. He liked to watch Jesusa as she told the story.

* * * * * * * * * * * * * * *

I first noticed Jesus on the day that he returned from the war. The soldiers came back very discouraged after the *norte americanos* had defeated them. The people of the village gathered in the streets cheering their safe return.

I stood with my sisters in a group of people, so at first I was not sure that Jesus was looking at me and smiling at me. But soon I realized that his eyes were following me. Flattered by his gaze, I waved and then walked over to join my sisters who had moved to a different place in the crowd. I was almost 18; he was older. His attention was very flattering.

The day after the soldiers returned, there was a fiesta thrown in their honor, and he asked me to dance. We danced several dances that evening. During the fiesta, as I talked with my sisters and watched the festivities, I noticed Jesus talking to my father. I was very curious about it.

Several days later I saw him from afar as he worked in the fields; I stopped to watch him work. He lifted his head as I watched and waved in my direction. I returned the wave with a smile and then returned to my tasks.

That evening while I warmed tortillas for dinner, I glanced up at the sound of footsteps. Jesus stood there with flowers in his hand. "Will you warm a few extra tortillas?" he asked smiling.

Flustered, I nodded and quickly turned back to the comal adding a few more tortillas. It was so easy to wave to him from afar, but when he was near me, I was tongue-tied. He walked with me into the house and my mamá just beamed. My parents exchanged a quick smile. That smile is a favorite memory of mine.

Jesus's manner was very confident and easy going. After dinner we walked to the plaza and he talked of politics and his hopes for the future. I felt safe with Jesus.

For several weeks, Jesus, sought me out and brought me flowers he picked in the grassy areas at the base of the mountains. Many nights he came to dinner. When there were fiestas, he danced with me.

One night after a fiesta...

★ ★ ★ ★ ★ ★ ★ ★ ★ ★ ★ ★ ★ ★ ★

"Clara, do you want to fill in what you remember before I continue?" Jesusa asked

"Maybe, or perhaps Jesus will do us the honor?" Clara looked at her son waiting for his answer.

"Yes, Mamá. I will tell this part of the story," Jesus replied. Previously Clara had always told this part of the story. Everyone watched as he stepped across the room. He stood behind Jesusa's chair and laid his hands on her shoulders. As he talked, the family listened intently.

★ ★ ★ ★ ★ ★ ★ ★ ★ ★ ★ ★ ★ ★ ★

My Jesusa was the most beautiful girl in the village. I did not think that she could love someone so old. I was 28; she was 17, almost 18. At the fiesta, I asked her father if I could call on her. He gave his approval and I began visiting often.

I knew from my first day back in the village that I wanted to marry Jesusa, but I waited to see if she wanted to marry me. At the beginning, I had hope. She stopped to wave if she saw me in the village, but when I visited her house the first time, she hardly spoke to me. Not until after dinner when we walked in the village did she begin to talk.

When I went home after visiting at her house, I told my parents that I wanted to marry Jesusa. My mamá cried tears of joy. I think she thought that I would never marry. My father, Jose, was very pleased.

He told me that Jesusa's father was a good man, and that Jesusa would make a good wife. "You chose well," he said and patted me on the back.

Mamá pulled out her treasured rebozo, the blue one that we have all heard about. "When you propose, give her this!" Mamá instructed. Her mamá had given it to her on her wedding day.

"Soon, Mamá. But first I want to know that she loves me."

For many weeks, I visited or danced with her at fiestas. We danced and talked, and I hoped. One night after a fiesta, while we walked I offered my arm and she slid her arm through mine. I laid my hand on top of hers. That hand, so delicate, so feminine.

"Don't you love our village? People here are happy." Jesusa commented as she watched people enjoying the evening.

"Would you ever leave the village?" I asked.

I will never forget her answer. She stopped and turned to face me. Quietly she said, "If you asked me to, I would go anywhere. I feel safe with you."

Then I knew. I asked her to wait for me right where she stood, and I ran to my house. She probably thought I was crazy. I was not gone long. She was patiently standing where I left her when I returned.

* * * * * * * * * * * * * * * *

Jesus patted Jesusa on the shoulder. "You finish our story." He kissed her on the top of her head and returned to his spot against the wall. Jesusa dabbed her eyes with her apron, then smoothed it out in her lap. "I think that is enough story for tonight."

As Petra was settling the children, she stopped and whispered to Francisco. "I need to talk to you tonight, outside, after the children are settled."

Francisco nodded and wandered outside to wait for her. The night air was humid and warm. There was no breeze to chase away the heat. It was awhile before the door opened and Petra stepped out onto the porch. "Let's walk. I do not want to talk on the porch."

He took her hand and they walked off the porch and away from house. The moon was almost full, and cast ample light on the ground to see the path. For several minutes the only sounds were the rhythm of their footsteps, the swishing of her skirt, and the choir of critters all around them. Francisco patiently waited until Petra was ready to speak. He was concerned because she looked upset. Surely she had not changed her mind.

Finally Petra spoke. "That day in the storm…" Sobs interrupted her words. She turned and buried her face in his chest.

Francisco was frantic. "What's wrong? Talk to me, Petra," he said, wrapping his arms around her.

"I am pregnant." Her sobs began again.

He held her even tighter and whispered in her ear, "Do not cry, Hermosa. Do not cry. All will be okay. I will protect you."

"How? October is still months away." Petra asked between sobs.

"Your dresses will hide it. And what does it matter to me? You are mine. This baby is mine. I love you, and I will take care of you. You are safe with me. Tomorrow I will ask Jesus if we can marry sooner."

Petra dried her tears and quieted herself. "No. We will keep the secret as long as we can."

Francisco held her close, whispered assurances, and stroked her hair. But soon his assurances turned into an apology. "I love you, Petra. I never meant to put you in this situation, or to sully your reputation. I just… I just…"

Petra touched her finger to his lips. "I know, Francisco."

※

The next morning Petra served breakfast, but was concerned when Clara did not come to the table. Petra walked into the room that they shared and found her still in bed.

"Abuelita, are you okay?" Petra asked.

"I am tired, tired and old. I just need to rest."

"May I bring you something to eat?" Petra asked, wiping her hands on her apron.

"Yes, a little something would be good." Clara said as she sat up in bed.

Petra hurried off to prepare a plate for her abuelita. She quickly returned with a plate of eggs and beans and a cup of coffee. "Here, Abuelita." Petra handed Clara the plate and placed the coffee on the table near her bedside.

"Thank you, Petra." She looked at Petra intently for several moments. "Will you always remember our story?"

Petra smiled. "I will always remember the story, but you will be here for many years to tell us the story."

Clara nodded and returned to her food.

"I am needed in the field today. Estefana will be here with the little ones. Just call to her if you need something," Petra said as she put on her bonnet.

Before walking out the door, she told Estefana to check on Clara often. Petra was concerned. She hurried out the door, picked up a sack from near the barn, and joined the others in the field picking cotton. For hours in the hot summer sun, they picked cotton. With so many in the field picking, they could fill a wagon today.

At lunchtime, they all went in and found Clara up and around, cooking a large pot of beans. After a lunch of beans and tortillas, they went back out to the field. Petra tucked a tortilla in her apron pocket for later.

At the end of the day Petra's hands were scratched and sore. Her body ached from bending and lugging the bag of cotton through the field. After dinner, everyone was tired and hurried off to bed. The story was forgotten until after the cotton was picked.

✳

Francisco rose early and hitched the horses to the wagon. The family had picked a wagonload of cotton the day before and he was preparing to haul the last wagonload of the season to the gin.

Petra walked out to the porch wiping her hands on the dishtowel draped over her shoulder. "Come in and eat something before you leave."

"Be there in a minute," he replied as he secured the load in the wagon.

She went back into the house and laid out a plate and utensils for him. The house was still quiet. They were the only two up and about, but soon everyone would be awake.

Francisco came in and sat at the table. Petra filled his plate with food and poured him a cup of coffee.

"Feeling okay?" he asked between bites.

She glanced around before she answered quietly, "Yes, most days."

When he finished eating, he grabbed his hat and kissed her. "See you at dinner." Then he walked outside, climbed into the wagon, and headed for the cotton gin.

Petra thought the day would be long without Francisco home, but once she began her daily chores the hours passed quickly.

※

Francisco arrived home just as the family sat down to dinner. He hung his hat by the door and took his seat next to Petra. "There's 1000 pounds of cotton seed in the wagon. The wagon is in the barn," he said.

"It will be fine there overnight. We'll pull out what we need to plant in the spring—for here and for your new place—then dump the rest in the river," Jesus responded.

Petra looked as Francisco with surprise. "New place?"

He nodded, his mouth full of food. After chewing he added, "Yes, after the wedding. I was going to tell you tonight. I just finalized things today while I was out. One of the sharecroppers here is moving away. We'll move into their cabin when they leave. And we'll be planting more acres."

After dinner they all gathered in the sitting room and asked Jesusa to continue the story. She obliged.

* * * * * * * * * * * * * * * *

Jesus asked me to wait, so I waited. It wasn't long before he returned, out of breath. "Jesusa," he said once he'd caught his breath, "Will you marry me?"

He was never one for extra words. Then he handed me the blue rebozo. "This was woven by my great grandmother. My mamá gave it to me to give to my bride. Will you accept?"

"Yes, Jesus, I will marry you."

He wrapped the rebozo around me and kissed me on the top of my head, then held my hand as we walked back to my house. I remember it like it was yesterday.

Wedding plans were made. We married in September. I had just turned eighteen. I wore my best china poblano. I only had two. The one I wore that day was a white colorfully embroidered top and a red skirt. I wore my hair pulled back and knotted with flowers tucked into my hair. My head was covered with the blue rebozo.

My family gathered and walked me to the church, cheering and laughing as we went. That was the custom. Walking through the dirt streets, I could hear Jesus and his family also making their way to the chapel. My brother ran up and gave me a handful of wildflowers. Padre Garza, the same priest that christened me, was standing at the front of the long white chapel and Jesus stood next to him dressed in his white cotton pants, and a new white shirt. My friend, Anastacia, was at the front as my witness. My papá walked me to the front. My bare feet made almost no noise on the hardened dirt aisle. At the front, Jesus and I knelt as the priest performed the rites of marriage. The lasso was put around us and the priest said the blessings. When he finished the ceremony, Jesus kissed me, but not on the top of my head. Then the bells chimed. Their ringing almost could not be heard above the cheers and congratulations.

Jesus and I walked out of the chapel followed by our family and friends. The music started. One friend played a guitar. Another sang. We wandered through the streets until we arrived in the small plaza, where friends had set up the reception. We'd made food for days before the reception. Somehow my papá even managed to buy a chicken for our wedding feast. The food was simple, but no one cared. It was a joyous day.

A year later, Porfiria was born.

* * * * * * * * * * * * * * * * *

"No more tonight." Jesusa said abruptly as she wiped tears from her eyes. She quickly said goodnight and left the room. Jesus followed her out.

No one asked what was wrong. They all knew. Porfiria and her younger sister, Manuela, died after the family arrived in Texas, and Jesusa still ached when either name was spoken. The family would wait for Jesusa to tell more of the story when she was ready.

Chapter 10
September 1880

For weeks, no one mentioned the story. Then one night in late September when the moon was full and the air was just beginning to cool, Jesusa asked if everyone would like to hear more of the story.

"Thank you, Jesusa," said Clara, "sad stories are important, too."

Jesusa nodded and began where she'd left off.

* * * * * * * * * * * * * * *

Porfiria was born a year later. She was independent and full of life. She spent her first year tied to my back in a rebozo. Not the blue one, that one I only wore on special days. When she could walk, she would follow me as I cooked, or cleaned, or worked in our little plot of land. She was not very old when I was expecting again. And then San Juana was born. We christened her Maria de San Juan.

* * * * * * * * * * * * * * * *

Petra handed her mother a handkerchief. She knew what part of the story was coming. Jesus left his chair in the kitchen and stood next to Jesusa with his hand resting on her shoulder. She looked up at him, patted his hand, and smiled.

* * * * * * * * * * * * * * * *

Jesus loved his little girls. We both loved them. One night as I was laying them down, I noticed that San Juana felt very warm to the touch. I called for Jesus to get some water and to call Mamá Gertrudis. She knew how to use the herbs to heal. Jesus came with the water then left with Porfiria. I did not want her to get sick also. Clara let Porfiria stay with her while we watched over San Juana. Mamá Gertrudis arrived with a handful of herbs. She crushed the herbs, mixed them, and added water. Carefully she had San Juana drink a little. Days went by, Mamá Gertrudis came and went, but instead of San Juana getting better, she got worse.

When I knew that her end was near, I told Mamá Gertrudis to go. Jesus was working in the field. No work meant no food. I was alone with my baby girl. I picked her up, held her in my arms, and sang to her as I paced back and forth in that little adobe house. I am not sure how long I paced, or even when she died. When Jesus walked in from the field, he knew. He fell to his knees, and for the first time, I saw tears run down his face. I walked over to him and laid my hand on his shoulder as he cried. After a few minutes he stood to his feet and held me, our little girl cuddled between us.

Grief is very hard to bear, but easier when it rests on two sets of shoulders. I was very thankful that I was not alone. San Juana was buried in the little cemetery in El Potosi. We scraped together the pesos to have the priest bless her burial.

My heart ached for a long time, but life continued. I still had my Porfiria, and she needed her mamá. About six months later, I was expecting again. Porfiria was almost four when little Jesus was born. Life was busy after he arrived! Three years later, Petra was born. Our little adobe house was as full as our hearts.

But during this time, things outside the village were changing, and some changes affected the way we lived. Other things, closer to the village, affected us, too. During that time some of the Indians that chose not to settle and take the ways of the Spanish, attacked the smaller villages around El Potosi.

I remember one night I was awakened by the sounds of men and horses. A small village nearby had been attacked and they were gathering men to go rescue whoever they could find and to discover what had happened. Jesus heard the next day that many were killed in the attack and that the Indians who attacked were hiding in the mountains. Our little village did not seem safe anymore.

One night just as we were all going to bed, Jesus asked me to walk with him. I made sure the children were settled, and we walked along the dirt street in front of our house.

"Our village is not like it used to be. In many ways it is not safe, and we have spent many months barely having enough to eat. I know that you go hungry some nights so that the children have enough."

I looked down waiting for him to continue.

"I have always owed money to the hacendado (hacienda owner) since returning from the war. Just when we would get a little extra, something would happen, and I would borrow again. But laws were passed and things have changed. Yesterday, I paid off my debt to the hacendado."

"Jesus, what are you saying?"

He pulled me close and was quiet for several moments before he spoke again. "Remember that night after the fiesta when you said that you would leave the village if I asked. Tonight I am asking, Jesusa. Here there will never be enough. We will always be hungry. Soon we will not have the Indian land to farm as our own. I think we should leave El Potosi."

His words hung in the air, heavy. I wiped at tears that persisted even though I willed them not to come. "Jesus, I will follow you anywhere. Will we go alone? Where will we go?"

"Saltillo. I was there during the war. It is a city much bigger than here. I can learn a trade. I do not know if we will go alone. I wanted to talk with you first. There are others that may want to go. I will talk with them."

After a few weeks of preparations, we packed up our few possessions and our children. There was no wagon, no burro, only us. I gathered the goods we were taking into bundles and tied them to our backs. Thankfully, we did not go alone. Jesus's parents, Clara and Jose, journeyed with us. So did Francisco and Lucio and their parents and siblings. Jesus's sister and her family, and his brother and his family also moved to Saltillo, but after we moved. And my sister and her family did also. They all journeyed together at a different time.

Our journey to Saltillo took about a week. Each day, we walked for hours in the morning, then stopped to eat a little something and rest for a while. After our rest, we walked until the light started to fade, and then we stopped, built a fire, and prepared dinner. After all that, we slept, and then got up the next morning and did it all again.

I had never been out of El Potosi. Jesus had told me stories about some of the places he saw during the war, but all of his stories could not have prepared me for what I saw when we cleared the top of the mountain ridge and looked down onto Saltillo. The city sits in a valley; the valley was full of adobe buildings. How would we ever make a life in a busy city? All we had ever known was farming.

✳ ✳ ✳ ✳ ✳ ✳ ✳ ✳ ✳ ✳ ✳ ✳ ✳ ✳ ✳

"If I talk much longer, we'll hear the rooster crow." Jesusa said.

Everyone went to bed, except Petra and Francisco. They went out to the porch. Francisco stood behind Petra and wrapped his arms around her letting his hands rest on her stomach. "I love you both," he whispered in her ear.

"No one has said anything, and I am not showing yet, perhaps our secret will remain so until the wedding. Only one more month," Petra said as she snuggled into his embrace.

Chapter 11
October 1880

The month passed quickly. Petra was glad for the quiet wedding they'd planned: a simple ceremony at the Justice of the Peace and a meal at the house. It was not at all elaborate, but given the circumstances, she was glad for that.

Thursday night, before the wedding, Petra and Francisco met on the porch as they often did. He handed her a small box. "For you," he said.

Petra lifted the top of the box and saw a hair comb nestled inside.

"I am sorry it is so little," mumbled Francisco, "But I thought you could use for your hair. I do not have…"

Petra interrupted him with a kiss. "You are more than enough, Francisco," she said and kissed him again. Then she ran her hand along the stubble of his cheek.

"It's perfect. I will wear it tomorrow."

❃

The next morning, Petra rose early to prepare breakfast. She lit the stove and then went out to feed the chickens while the stove heated. When she walked back into the house, her mother was in the kitchen.

"Good Morning, Petra," said Jesusa.

"Good morning, Mamá."

"We are very happy for you and Francisco. I will be sorry to see you leave, but it will be easier for you in your own place," Jesusa said. "Are you happy, Petra?"

"Yes, Mamá, very happy. Francisco loves me, and I love him."

They prepared breakfast, served the family, and did their daily chores. Soon it was time for them to get ready for the wedding. Petra dressed her boys. They each looked so handsome in their shorts, dress shirt, and jacket. She dressed Candida in the white cotton dress that she made for her. A deep blue sash accented the waist and tied in the back. Petra sent them out to the sitting room to put shoes on their feet.

"Ask your uncles to help you if you need it," She called as they scrambled out of the room.

Petra laid out her long, cream-colored, ruffled skirt and an off-white muslin bodice that buttoned up the front. She had tried them on to be sure they still fit. Thankfully, they did. She took off her apron and her calico dress. Over her drawers and chemise, she tied her bustle and corset.

Estefana peeked in "Need any help?"

"Yes, could you help with my corset?"

"Sure," Estefana replied, already starting to cinch up the waist.

"Not too tight! I want to breathe," said Petra.

Estefana finished up and left to check the food. Petra slid into her petticoat, then her skirt, fastening it and smoothing it out over the petticoat and bustle. She pulled on the bodice and buttoned the small pearlescent buttons. Satisfied that everything looked right, she moved on to her hair.

She brushed it out, then she swept it up into a twist and held it in place with her new hair comb. She used her finger to curl the hairs the dangled around her cheeks and forehead. As she finished, she heard horses. Francisco and Lucio were headed to town.

Not long after they left, Petra, her parents, and her children loaded into the wagon. Josefa and Estefana waved from the porch, and Petra's younger brothers waved from the barn as the wagon pulled away.

Lucio and Francisco were waiting for them on the steps of the courthouse. Earlier in the month, Petra and Francisco had gotten a marriage license. So today they went directly to Judge Wells. In a simple ceremony they exchanged vows and promised to love "'til death do them part." Petra's parents stood as witnesses. Candida and her brothers clapped and cheered when they heard "man and wife." The happy couple kissed amidst congratulations.

※

Estefana and Josefa had the food ready and the table set when everyone returned. They all sat and enjoyed the food. After a while, Jesus cleared his throat, a signal that he wanted to speak. He raised his glass and said, "To Francisco, you married well! And to Petra, may your future be filled with love." Glasses were raised in agreement.

※

Petra went into the bedroom to pack up the last of her things. She closed her trunk and looked around the room. Clara, Estefana, and Josefa would have more room in here now. She looked out the window and watched as the guys pulled the wagon up in front, then heard footsteps on the porch as they came in to get the trunk.

Once it was loaded, Francisco lifted her into the wagon and then hoisted himself up next to her. Petra waved as they pulled away. The children were staying with her parents for a night or two while she set up the new house. The wagon seemed almost silly for such a short distance, but it was too far to carry her trunk by hand.

In the weeks leading up to the wedding, they had cleaned the house and aired it out. Now it became their home. Petra waited in the wagon while Lucio helped Francisco carry the trunk into the house. Once they finished Lucio waved and walked back to his cabin.

Francisco helped Petra down from the wagon and they went into the cabin. He wrapped his arms around her and said, "For years I dreamed that we would marry and that you would be mine. Today my dreams have come true."

Chapter 12
February 1881

Francisco and Petra settled into married life easily. He worked in the fields. She kept the house and cared for the children. As the weeks passed, her middle expanded and their secret was a secret no longer.

The news of the coming baby was temporarily overshadowed by other news. Lucio and Estefana announced their plans to marry. Petra wondered if someone else had a secret to keep. She talked to Estefana about it.

"Estefana, I am very happy for you, but you are very young, only fourteen. Are you keeping a secret?"

Estefana laughed and pointed to Petra's belly. "No, Petra, no secrets. Lucio has an opportunity to work some land only a few miles from here. Having a wife will make that much easier. I love Lucio and want to help him. Lucio loves me, too."

Petra hugged her sister. "I hope you are both very happy."

※

Petra waddled around her kitchen preparing a meal. The family was coming to her house after the wedding ceremony to celebrate. The sound of the wagon signaled their arrival. Francisco patted his brother on the back as he came in the door.

"Congratulations! Come in! Come in!" Francisco welcomed the guests. "Petra has been cooking all day. If it tastes as good as it smells, we are all in for a treat."

"Best Wishes, Estefana!" Petra said as she hugged her sister. "Congratulations, Lucio. We are so happy for you."

The entire family was there. Even Jesus, Urbana, and their family had come up for the day. Everyone enjoyed a tasty meal and great company. After the meal, the happy couple loaded into their wagon, and Lucio whisked his bride away to their new home, a few miles away. After their departure, everyone settled inside and since so many were together, it seemed a good time to tell a small part of the story.

* * * * * * * * * * * * * * * *

Life in Saltillo was hard. Jose and Clara lived with us which helped a lot. Jesus and Jose worked very hard to keep us all fed. We moved around quite a bit, usually staying in inns or boarding houses. Sometimes the room where we lived had no space for cooking so we bought most of our meals from the street vendors. It is hard to eat others' food when you know that Clara's food tastes so much better.

It was nice having them live with us. Clara often watched the children while I cleaned houses. We were thankful they made the move with us.

At that time, even in our poverty, we were happy. Life was full of new experiences and our family was growing. Manuela was born not long after we moved to Saltillo. Josefa was born two years later. Austacio and Gregorio followed in the years after that.

After Gregorio was born we moved to Meson de Belen. In that place we had such nice neighbors.

* * * * * * * * * * * * * * *

"I want to wait until Estefana is with us to tell the next part of this story. It is part of her story." Jesusa said as she wiped a tear. "And it is still very hard to talk about my children who are now with God."

It was more than a month before the family was gathered and Jesusa continued the story.

Chapter 13
March 1881

When Petra could tell that soon she would be holding her new baby, she talked to Francisco, and they came up with a plan. Josefa would stay with them until it was time for the baby to be born. When it was time for the baby's arrival, Josefa would take the little ones and go to her parents' cabin.

Late one afternoon, Petra felt the familiar pains that told her it was time. She sent Josefa into the field to call Francisco.

"Petra said it is time," said Josefa, breathless from running.

Francisco dropped his tools and began to run. "Josefa, you take Alcario, Samuel, and Candida and go back to your house." Without waiting for a response, he ran off toward the house in a full run. Josefa walked as fast as she could, trying to catch her breath.

Francisco ran into the house and found Petra lying on the bed. "I am all right, Francisco, but please fetch the midwife."

Francisco leaned over and kissed her forehead. "Be back soon." He jumped up and ran out the door.

Josefa arrived back at the house just as Francisco galloped away on his horse. She gathered the children and let Petra know they were leaving. Thankfully the other cabin was not far away. Josefa carried Candida. Samuel and Alcario ran alongside her.

Francisco did not have to wait long for the midwife. After he told her that she was needed, she hitched her wagon and headed to the cabin. They had barely stopped in front when the midwife was out of the wagon and in the front door. Francisco tied up the horses and walked into the house. He was in the house only a few minutes then he walked back outside.

He did everything he could do to make life comfortable for his Petra, but in this, he could offer no help or comfort. He paced outside. It seemed hours; although, it was not very long before Jesus and Jesusa arrived. Jesusa hugged Francisco and then walked into the house. Jesus quietly began to pace with Francisco.

Several minutes passed before Jesus broke the silence, "It doesn't get any easier."

For hours they paced. Jesusa brought them coffee, but they remained outside. The sun sank toward the horizon as the hours passed. At twilight, Jesusa stepped out onto the porch. "Francisco, come in."

Hurriedly, he walked up the steps and in the front door. He ran to Petra and saw her sitting up in bed holding a bundle.

"It's a girl," said Petra. "What shall we name her?"

"She's beautiful, just like you, Hermosa. What about Maria?" Francisco wiped a tear from Petra's cheek as he responded.

"I like that name. We'll call her Maria," agreed Petra.

Jesus and Jesusa told them that they would keep the other children with them for a few days so that Petra could rest. They said their goodbyes and walked back home. The midwife climbed into her wagon and drove home with her chicken and a few coins as payment.

Petra smiled up at Francisco. "Would you like to hold her?"

"I do not know if … I am afraid I'll break her. She seems so small and fragile."

Petra patted the bed next to her. "Come and sit."

Francisco sat on the bed, and she placed little Maria in his arms. "She looks like you, Petra," he said.

Petra smiled. These were the moments that would be added to her story. Seeing Francisco holding their baby stirred her heart. "I am not sure how much more love this heart of mine can hold."

Francisco winked at her. "I am so happy that I may cry," he said.

Petra wiped her tears and laughed.

※

On a Sunday when Maria was about two weeks old, the entire family gathered at Jesusa's house. Many in the family met baby Maria for the first time that afternoon. After a lively and satisfying dinner, Estefana asked Jesusa to continue the story. She happily obliged.

* * * * * * * * * * * * * *

When we lived in Meson de Belen, the Losanos lived next door. Their daughter was about a year younger then Gregorio. Sometimes their daughter would stay with us when the Losanos were both working. Such a nice family.

* * * * * * * * * * * * * * * *

Lucio put his arm around Estefana and handed her his handkerchief. She leaned her head against his shoulder and wiped her tears.

* * * * * * * * * * * * * * * *

One day Gregorio had a fever. All the heartache of losing San Juana came pouring back as I cared for Gregorio. But there was nothing I could do. One night the fever became too much for his little body to fight, and he simply stopped breathing. With so many other children, I was very busy—which left little time to mourn—but the heartache was still there. Parents should never have to bury their children.

A few days later, the Losanos apologetically asked if we could again watch their little girl while they worked. She was no trouble, and we never minded having her with us. Oddly, they did not return that night, or the next night, which was very unusual. A week went by before we found out what had happened. There was an accident. I do not know the details, but they were both killed. They had no other family, so the little girl that they left with us became ours, our little Estefana.

Only weeks after the Losano's accident, Ignacio was born. By then we had moved to Meson de San Julian. We *stayed there for a while. When Ignacio was about two, Plutarco was born."*

* * * * * * * * * * * * * * * *

Little Maria began to fuss. "I think it is time we go," said Petra.

"Thank you for coming." Jesusa replied. She loved it when her family gathered together.

Chapter 14
January 1882

The morning was cold. Frost covered the ground. Petra and Francisco loaded into the wagon and went to the church for the christening of their little Maria. Petra held Maria on her lap and slid close to Francisco. They'd waited until she was almost a year old hoping to avoid uncomfortable questions from the priest. The other children were with Petra's family. They would all gather for a meal after the christening.

The priest performed the christening, but made no mention of a discrepancy in dates. After the christening, the entire family gathered in Jesusa's kitchen for a family dinner, and it seemed the perfect time for Jesusa to continue the story.

* * * * * * * * * * * * * * * *

While we were living in Saltillo, Mexico was having trouble. The French came to Mexico and set up a king. Benito Juarez and his armies were fighting them to save our Mexico. Jesus, my oldest son, had strong opinions and often spoke out in favor of President Juarez. More than once this got him into trouble. I tried to tell him that it was dangerous, but he would not be silenced. The hardest day was when he came running toward me calling that he was being sought by the soldiers and he needed to hide.

Desperate to save my son, I had to think fast. I could not outsmart the fevers that had taken my other children, but I was not going to let the federales get my oldest son so easily. Trying to think of places they would not look, I called for him to follow me hoping inspiration would come as I started moving. Then I thought of the pigs. No one liked being around the pigs. I instructed him to hide in the pig sty. It worked. They searched for hours and never found him.

Thankfully soon after that things changed. The French were defeated. President Juarez was reelected. But those years in Saltillo were hard. Very hard. There were good things that happened. Our son, Jesus, learned a trade. He learned to make shoes and sold them on the street. Estefana joined our family. Despite the hardships, many happy memories were made in Saltillo.

* * * * * * * * * * * * * * *

Jesusa stood on the porch waving as Petra and her family walked back to their cabin and the others pulled away in their wagons. She loved that her children lived near. Jesus walked up behind her and slid his arms around her. They quietly stood listening to the chirping crickets and watching the moon rise.

"Who knew that the road out of El Potosi would lead us here?" mused Jesus.

"It seems so far away. A lifetime ago, but these are the happiest days yet."

The months that followed brought even more happiness. Petra was expecting again. The family continued to grow.

Chapter 15
March 1883

Petra watched Francisco walk out to the field and rubbed her expanding middle. Her baby could come any day now. She smiled as she remembered Francisco's reaction when she told him another baby was on the way.

Several days later Petra woke Francisco in the early hours of the morning. Even the rooster was still asleep. "Please go get the midwife and let Mamá know that it is time," she said before another contraction silenced her temporarily.

Francisco jumped out of bed, dressed quickly, and ran out the door. He saddled a horse and rode to the nearby cabin to tell Jesusa. He ran up the steps and knocked quietly at the door. Jesus answered.

"The baby is coming. I am going to get the midwife."

"Thank you. I'll tell Jesusa," replied Jesus.

Francisco mounted his horse and galloped away. An hour later, when he returned with the midwife right behind him in her wagon, Jesusa met him on the porch, smiling.

"He did not wait for you," Jesusa said.

"He?" Francisco asked as he dismounted his horse. "How is Petra?"

"Come and see for yourself," said Jesusa opening the door.

Francisco walked in but waited by the bedroom door while the midwife tended to Petra and the baby. It was not long before the midwife handed Francisco a small bundle.

He walked over to Petra's bedside. Jesusa and the midwife slipped quietly out of the room.

"He needs a name. What do you want to name him?" Francisco asked.

"Francisco," Petra said. "He is my little Francisco."

Alcario, Samuel, Candida, and little Maria were thrilled when they awoke to the news of a baby brother. In the following weeks, family and friends that visited all said that the little one looked just like his father. Francisco beamed with pride. Petra had given him a son.

Chapter 16
February 1884

The sound of a knock at the door woke Jesusa. She put on her robe and hurried to the door. Francisco slipped in as soon as the door opened. "It's Samuel. He's gotten worse. Petra has been awake with him all night. Can you come?"

"Give me only a minute." Jesusa said as she walked into the other room. She walked out moments later with her shoes in her hand and her coat over her arm.

"Jesus will bring my other things later," she said as she put on her shoes. "Let's go."

In her nightgown and coat, she followed Francisco to the cabin, hurried along by fear. "His fever is worse?"

"Yes." Francisco was using as few words as possible in order to maintain his composure. He feared the worst. Jesusa ran to the door.

Samuel was in the small bed in his parents' bedroom. Normally the younger children slept there. Jesusa could see the concern in Petra's eyes. "He's very hot, Mamá. What should I do? He is not yet even seven years old. I cannot lose him." Petra was wiping his head with a wet rag hoping it would bring down his fever.

"You go rest. I will tend to him while you rest and will wake you if things get much worse." Jesusa clutched the rag and began wiping with Samuel's head. She urged Francisco to rest also. He and Petra laid down. Exhausted, Petra fell asleep quickly. Francisco tried to sleep, but sleep never came. Soon the sun was breaking over the horizon and the world outside started to stir. He was awake. He got up quietly and asked Jesusa if she needed anything.

Jesusa whispered, "He is very ill. He needs to be blessed by the priest."

Francisco grabbed his coat and was out the door. An hour later, he returned alone. "The priest will not come," he said. "He thinks the risk it too great. He sends his blessing, but will not come."

Jesusa shook her head. Samuel's breathing had become very shallow.

"It is time to wake Petra. I do not think he will be with us much longer," Jesusa whispered through tears.

Francisco went to Petra and stroked her hair hoping to wake her gently, but she sat upright and asked, "Is he…?"

"He's still alive, but you best go to him. He's getting worse," Francisco said.

Sobs caught in her throat as she ran to her son. Jesusa left her alone with Samuel and gathered the other children. Candida, Alcario, and Maria were awake, and little Francisco was crying. She sat them in the kitchen and made breakfast. Francisco stood helpless in the bedroom doorway.

"Francisco, go to her. She needs you," Jesusa said as she added beans to the scrambled egg and stirred it in the pan.

Francisco quietly stepped in the room. Petra was sitting on the floor holding Samuel, her face turned away from the door. Francisco knelt next to her and laid a hand on her shoulder. "Is he..?" She looked at him, and when he saw her face, he knew the answer. "Oh, Petra..." he said, but sobs took over for words. He wrapped his arms around them both and cried.

Jesusa struggled to serve the food and remain calm for the other children. The sound of familiar footsteps at the front door announced Jesus's arrival.

"Abuelo! Tia Josefa!" Candida said as they came through the door. Jesus read the news on Jesusa's face and quietly asked Josefa to finished feeding the children. He motioned for Jesusa to join him on the porch.

Jesusa whispered to Josefa as she walked toward the door, "The children have not been told."

As soon as the front door closed, Jesusa buried her face in Jesus's shoulder and cried, not just for the loss of her grandson, but for the pain that her daughter was suffering. Jesusa knew the hurt that Petra felt and ached for her daughter.

Josefa finished feeding the children and then tenderly explained why their mamá was crying. Nine year old, Alcario got up from the table and ran out to the porch.

Jesus handed Jesusa the clothes that he'd brought for her and then turned his attention to his grandson. Jesus walked over and leaned on the porch rail next to Alcario. After several minutes of silence, Jesus said, "It hurts to say goodbye. You do not have to be strong all the time." He could see Alcario fighting back tears and handed him his handkerchief. "It is okay to let out the tears. Wait out here. We'll be back out in a few minutes." He squeezed his shoulder and turned toward the door.

"But you are always strong, Abuelo," Alcario said.

"No. Not always," Jesus replied, without turning around. He wiped his eyes with his sleeve and walked back into the house.

Jesusa changed her clothes, and wiped her face. Jesus was holding baby Francisco and Josefa was putting shoes on Maria when she walked into the sitting room. Before leaving, she went to the bedroom to say goodbye. "Petra, we are taking the children to our house. The funeral should be tomorrow. You cannot wait too long. There is food on the stove."

Petra nodded, but did not move. Francisco walked over and thanked Jesusa.

❋

Hardly a word was spoken between Petra and Francisco for an hour or so. Petra sat with her son, then dressed him in his

Sunday best, and wept. After a while, Francisco coaxed her to the table. "You must eat, Petra. You have another baby to think about."

"Yes, you are right," she answered, rubbing her belly.

While they were eating, Francisco started to tell stories of things that Samuel had done or said. Petra looked up and took his hand. "Thank you." He kissed her hand and then finished his food.

After the meal, he excused himself. "I need to go take care of some things," he said as he got up to leave. "I'll be back in a few hours." He hated to leave Petra alone, but he knew that preparations for tomorrow must be made. He was glad to see his sister-in-law, Estefana, arrive just as he was walking out.

"How is she?" Estefana asked.

"Distraught," answered Francisco. "I am glad you are here. She needs someone near right now. I am going to prepare the grave for tomorrow."

Estefana went into the house and spent the afternoon sitting with Petra. Soon the house would be full of mourners and well-wishers, but while they sat it was silent except for the sound of Petra's wails.

Alone, Francisco was free to express his grief. He tried to be strong for Petra, but now his tears flowed freely as he dug the grave. Samuel would be buried next to his father.

※

The family all gathered the next day, loaded into wagons, and rode out to the grave site. After a brief and tearful ceremony, a long afternoon of sharing memories kept the family together until dinner. Josefa spent her afternoon preparing enough food for the family. Jesusa asked if she could continue the story. Petra nodded her consent.

✶ ✶ ✶ ✶ ✶ ✶ ✶ ✶ ✶ ✶ ✶ ✶ ✶ ✶

Goodbyes are very hard. We'd lived in Saltillo about twelve years. Then one day Jesus came home and asked me to walk with him after dinner. Once we were alone, he explained that he had talked with a man from Texas. The man offered to buy us a covered-wagon and pay for our travel, if we would work his land. "Years ago I asked you to leave El Potosi. Now I am asking you to leave Mexico," Jesus said.

I took his hands in mine and gave him the same response that I'd given him years before, "Jesus, I will follow you anywhere."

The man from Texas bought a wagon, and we packed up our belongings.

Francisco and Lucio said goodbye to their parents. We said goodbye to our family and friends and began our journey. It was difficult to say goodbye to those that we loved.

As we neared the border we grew concerned that our oldest son, Jesus, would not be able to cross without issue. He had made a name for himself. We also heard that unless you had paid for the military exemption, you could not leave Mexico until you served. We had no money for the exemption, so we came up with a different plan. We put our son, Jesus, in a dress!

We draped the blue rebozo over his head. He sat with Clara and me in the back of the wagon and simply smiled when we crossed the border.

The journey from Saltillo took us more than 40 days. And now our life is here, and we are still making our story.

* * * * * * * * * * * * * * * *

That signaled the end of the gathering. Tears were shed as hugs and condolences were exchanged. Once they were alone, Francisco simply held Petra. Her parents had taken the other children for the night. Her tears had run out, all that was left was silence and ache.

It seemed like weeks before Francisco saw Petra smile again. But her smiles were short-lived.

Chapter 17
July 1884

Petra sat up in bed abruptly.

"What's wrong?" Francisco asked sleepily.

"A bad dream, a very bad dream!"

"What was it?"

"Not before breakfast. I'll tell you tomorrow. Now, go back to sleep. I'm sorry I woke you." Petra knew not to tell her bad dreams before breakfast. It was bad luck. And this was a dream she hoped would never come true.

There was no time after breakfast to talk about dreams. Cleaning, chores, and work needed to be done. Francisco tapped her belly as he walked out the door and she could hear him whistling as he walked down toward the barn. Any day now there would be one more little one added to their family.

Petra cleaned up after breakfast and sent Alcario and Candida off to school. Francisco and Maria played on the porch while Petra did chores around the house. At nap time, she picked up Francisco and settled him down to sleep. Then she went back to Maria and found her asleep on the porch. Petra picked her up and carried her inside. The heat of a fever radiated off her body. Petra could not hold back tears. The memory of Samuel's recent death engulfed her as she wet a rag and began wiping Maria's head.

When Alcario and Candida arrived home from school, she sent Alcario to get Jesusa. "Go get Abuela! Tell her Maria is sick with fever."

When Francisco arrived home for dinner, he found Petra caring for Maria and Jesusa making supper. No words were exchanged. The fear in Petra's eyes told him all he needed to know.

After supper, Jesus arrived and took Jesusa and the other children back to their home. Hopefully, they could keep the fever from spreading to the others. Petra prayed that God would protect the little one inside her. For two day Petra cared for Maria hoping that her fever would break.

One evening, Francisco lit candles as the light started to fade, and their vigil continued. A knock at the door startled them both. Francisco answered the door. "Reverend Robertson, how are you?"

"Good evening. Please, call me Elias. I heard your daughter was sick. May I come in and pray with you?"

"Yes, of course." Francisco replied, surprised, stepping aside to let him enter. He could not help but remember the priest who would not come months ago.

Petra welcomed him and thanked him for coming, but she never left Maria's side. Reverend Elias prayed for little Maria, talking to God as a friend and Father. He asked for healing for Maria and for protection for Petra's unborn baby. His manner of praying was new to Petra. In her heart she echoed his prayers. He sat with them for more than an hour, sometimes silently, sometimes reading from the Bible, or offering words of comfort.

When he rose to leave, Francisco walked him out. "Reverend, I mean, Elias, how can I talk to God as you do? How can I know him as you do?" Francisco asked.

Reverend Elias opened his Bible and read to him from the book of Isaiah "Look unto me, and be ye saved." (Isaiah 45:22) and then from the book of Romans. "If you confess with your mouth that Jesus is Lord and believe in your heart that God raised Him from the dead, you will be saved." (Romans 10:9) Francisco listened intently as Elias explained what the verses meant. Then Elias handed Francisco his Bible and shook his hand. Francisco thanked him for coming and walked back into the house clutching the Bible.

He sat down next to Petra, opened the Bible to the pages that Elias had marked and read to her what he learned from the reverend. Together they prayed.

Little Maria died later that night. Petra wept. Francisco cradled the Bible and prayed for comfort.

※

Early the next morning, Francisco dug another grave, while Petra dressed her little girl and readied her for burial. The family gathered again and said goodbye to another little one.

Chapter 18
August 1884

Alcario and Candida walked into the cabin after returning from school and found Petra in the sitting room, bent over in pain.

"I am glad you two are home." Petra said as her contraction let up allowing her to speak. "The baby is coming. Alcario, please go tell the midwife. Candida, please take little Francisco to Abuela's house and stay with him there."

Alcario hurried off, and Candida took little Francisco over to Jesusa's. The midwife wasted no time in getting there. Thankfully this little one waited until after she arrived to make his appearance.

Francisco was out in the fields and did not return to the house until his work was done. When he returned, he ran into the house. "Are they both okay?" he asked.

"Petra and your son are fine," said the midwife.

Francisco ran to the bedroom and stood in the doorway smiling. Petra motioned him over to the bed.

"What will we name him?" Petra asked as she handed Francisco his son.

"Elias," said Francisco without hesitation. He would never forget the man that spent hours with them during their vigil and brought them comfort. "We will name him Elias."

※

Days later, they all gathered at Jesusa's place again.

"Abuelita, this is Elias." Petra said laying her bundle in Clara's arms.

"Precioso!" Clara cooed. "So many stories will be lived by these little ones."

Francisco agreed. "We are looking forward to many years of making stories."

Chapter 19
October 1884

Petra was awakened by the same terrible dream. Panic engulfed her. She snuggled close to Francisco and laid her head against his chest. The sound of his heartbeat brought her comfort. "Please do not leave me, Francisco," she whispered. "I need you here with me." She lay nestled against him until sleep found her again.

Hours later the morning dawned bright and clear. After breakfast, everyone scattered to their tasks. As Francisco walked toward the door, Petra called to him, "Wait!"

"Yes?"

"A proper goodbye!" Petra laughed as she walked over and kissed him.

He wrapped his arms around her and held her tight. "I love you, Hermosa! I'll be back in a few hours," he said with a wink and walked away whistling.

Petra set to work on her daily chores. Alcario and Candida were at school, and the two younger boys were home with Petra. She sang as she worked. Despite recent heartaches, joy was growing in her heart again.

※

The food bubbling on the stove smelled delicious. She hoped Francisco would be home soon. She looked out the window and was surprised to see her father and Lucio riding toward her cabin.

She walked out to greet them. "I have hot food on the stove. Come in for…" she stopped mid-sentence when she saw her father's face. "Where's Francisco?"

"I am so sorry, Mija," Jesus began, "He was thrown from his horse and badly hurt." When he could not continue, Lucio spoke, "We hurried for a doctor, but it was too late."

"Where's Francisco?" Petra almost screamed. Only then did she see the wagon approaching. She ran to the wagon. Her brother, Austacio, mumbled condolences as she dashed to the back of the wagon and pulled back the blanket.

Francisco was dead.

Petra collapsed to the ground and wept. Minutes later, she felt a hand on her shoulder. She wiped her tears and composed herself. Her father offered his hand and helped her to her feet. She determined in her heart to be strong. Her children needed that. There would be time later for tears.

"Bring him inside please. We can lay him in the sitting room. Then, I will get you something to eat. Austacio, please see if Reverend Elias is in the area and tell him what happened," Petra said. She prayed quietly as Francisco was laid out in the house. Soon the house would be full of people. She busied herself serving food to her father and Lucio.

"Lucio, I am so sorry. He was not only mine. He was your brother," Petra said as she poured them both a cup of coffee.

"Thank you, Petra," Lucio choked out the words, fighting back tears.

The news of Francisco's death spread quickly. The house filled with people bringing food and offering their deepest sympathies.

Petra walked out to the porch knowing that Alcario and Candida would soon be home from school. She hoped that they had not heard the news. She saw them walking up the path and walked out to meet them.

"Hi, Mamá," said Candida.

Alcario noticed all the wagons and horses and commented, "Mamá, there are many people at the cabin."

Petra put her arms around them and pulled them close. "Papá was badly hurt…"

"Will he be all right?" interrupted Candida.

"No," Petra said, crying, "He…"

Alcario said the words that Petra could not utter. "Candida, Papá died."

Candida wailed, and Petra held her. Alcario stood up tall and put his arms around both of them.

"I will take care of you," said Alcario.

"Thank you, Alcario." Petra said and leaned her head against his.

Petra's heart ached for her children. Alcario and Candida had already lost one father. Francisco was a wonderful papá to them. And his two little boys were so young. Right now they could not even understand that he was gone. How would they remember him? She would be sure that they remembered. Stories. She would tell them the stories.

Late that afternoon Lucio went out and dug his brother's grave. When he was finished digging, he had no tears left to cry, just a deep ache.

The next day Reverend Elias joined the family at the graveside. He read from the Bible, said a few words of comfort, and prayed. Petra was thankful that he was there. And again, the family gathered for a meal. This gathering was even more subdued than after the last burials.

There was little conversation, mostly murmurs. No one knew what to say. Petra surprised them all when she spoke. Everyone listened as she began slowly. "Abuelita says that our story continues. So I am going to tell more of our story. Stories keep memories alive."

Clara wiped tears from her eyes and nodded. Petra continued.

* * * * * * * * * * * * * * * *

When we arrived in Texas, we had very little. The first year here was very difficult. We lost Abuelito Jose only weeks after we arrived. Then only a few months later, Porfiria and Manuela became very ill. They were so sick and succumbed so quickly. They died within days of each other.

After we were in Texas about two years, Mr. Torres met with my father and asked for my hand in marriage. He was much older. I barely knew him, but he needed a wife. We married. He was good to me. Alcario was born a year after we married, Samuel two years after that, and Candida the year following.

Mr. Torres was a good man. He helped people whenever he could. One day he helped the wrong person. A stranger asked for a ride and Mr. Torres let him ride behind him on his horse.

* * * * * * * * * * * * * * *

The room was silent as Petra silently sobbed and then composed herself enough to continue. With tears still streaming down her face, she began again.

* * * * * * * * * * * * * * *

The stranger took him from me. My Mr. Torres died. I felt alone, but my family was with me. Not just my family, but also my very good friends.

Then when I least expected it, I fell in love. The day was stormy. The clouds cleared, and I wanted to go to town. Francisco offered to drive me in the wagon. On our way into town, we were caught in a downpour, but on that day, I was most surprised by the flood of words—words of love and promise—that poured from Francisco.

He loved me.

* * * * * * * * * * * * * * *

Petra sobbed. Jesus stood and announced. "Enough stories for tonight."

"No, Papá. I want to finish. Sad stories are important, too."
"All right, Mija."
Petra fingered the comb in her hair before she continued.

* * * * * * * * * * * * * * * *

Francisco loved me. I felt safe with him always. The night before we married, he gave me a hair comb. I wear it almost every day. He worked hard to provide for his family. He was a great papá to all of my children. He was with me during the hardest days—on the days that I said goodbye to my children. Until now, I thought those were the hardest days.

When my Francisco died, my heart was torn in two. I do not know how my story continues without him. I do not even know how I can wake in the morning to a life without him.

* * * * * * * * * * * * * * * *

Jesus stood again and said, "It is late. We need to let Petra rest. If you want to help, come back tomorrow. We'll pack up Petra's belongings and bring her home."

After a flurry of hugs and tears, all was quiet. Petra put the children to bed and crawled into her own bed alone. She heard Alcario quietly crying. She knew that he hoped she would not hear him. He tried to be so strong for her. After a little while, he was quiet, and she prayed that he would sleep peacefully.

Sleep evaded her, so she continued to pray. As she lay there praying, she remembered the Bible that Reverend Elias had given to Francisco. He always kept it in a safe place. She went and picked it up, cradling it in her arms. She did not even know what verses to read so she pulled the Bible close to her chest and prayed. She cradled the Bible and prayed until sleep was her companion.

The next day their belongings were packed, and Petra with her four children moved back into her parents' cabin again.

Chapter 20
November 1884

The days that followed were long and painful. There were so many things that reminded Petra of Francisco. She loved the memories of him, but each memory brought a new flood of tears.

After the death of Mr. Torres, she worried for her future. Now she worried for her heart. Every day was spent learning how to live without Francisco. Alcario was especially attentive to his mamá. Candida was a help with young Francisco and little Elias. Again Petra's family carried her through the hardest of days.

One Sunday morning, Jesus told everyone to put on their best clothes. He went out to hitch the horses to the wagon. When everyone was ready to go, the entire family piled into the wagon.

Alcario asked what most everyone was wondering. "Where are we going?"

"To a church meeting," Jesusa answered.

After a short ride, Jesus pulled to a stop near a farmhouse where a group of ten or more families were gathered near the porch. A few people were on the porch or seated on benches or chairs just off the porch. Others were standing in the grass in front of the house.

Petra and her family climbed down from the wagon and walked toward the meeting. Jesus led them to a place near the porch. Someone offered chairs to Petra and Jesusa. Petra took a seat and listened as the people began to sing. The words of the song reached out to her. Tears began to flow as she sang along with them.

<blockquote>
When peace like a river
attendeth my way,
When sorrows like sea billows roll
Whatever my lot,
Thou hast taught me to say,
It is well, It is well with my soul.
</blockquote>

Petra had never seen the sea, but she understood the sorrow described. "Oh, God," she prayed quietly, "make it well with my soul." After several more songs, Reverend Elias stood on the porch and began quoting Psalm 23.

Psalm 23

The Lord is my shepherd;
I shall not want.
He maketh me to lie down in green pastures:
he leadeth me beside the still waters.
He restoreth my soul:
He leadeth me in the paths of righteousness
for his name's sake.
Yea, though I walk through the valley
of the shadow of death,
I will fear no evil: for thou art with me;
thy rod and thy staff they comfort me.
Thou preparest a table before me
in the presence of mine enemies:
thou anointest my head with oil;
my cup runneth over.
Surely goodness and mercy shall follow me
all the days of my life, and
I will dwell in the house of the Lord forever.

"He restoreth my soul… Thy rod and staff comfort me." These words Petra committed to memory as Reverend Elias expounded on the meaning of the passage. The church meeting wrapped up a while later with another song. On the way home, Petra listened as the others talked about the sermon.

That night as Petra lay in bed, she prayed. "Father God, please make it well with my soul. My heart hurts, and my soul feels empty. Please restore my soul. I need your comfort."

Over the next several months, when Reverend Elias was preaching nearby, they would all attend. Slowly life became easier and the memories of Francisco brought more joy than sorrow. In spite of the ache that would forever be in her heart, Petra was joyful and looked forward to what lay ahead.

Chapter 21
July 1885

Petra rose early and helped her mother make breakfast. Soon the kitchen was full of people, but Clara was not at the table. After everyone was served, Petra hurried to the bedroom to wake her abuelita for breakfast. "Good morning, Abuelita, it is time for breakfast."

"Good morning, Petra. No breakfast for me today. Come and sit." Petra sat down on the edge of the bed. "It is your turn, Petra. You are going to be the keeper of the stories."

Confused by what Clara was saying, Petra answered quickly, "You are here to tell us the stories."

"No, Petra, it is your turn." Clara tapped Petra on the hand. Then she closed her eyes and passed into eternity. Tears flooded Petra's eyes. Slowly she walked back into the kitchen unsure how to break the news to the family.

"Is Clara awake?" Jesusa asked without looking up.

"No, Mamá. Abuelita is…" Petra began to sob. Jesus jumped up from the table and ran to the bedroom. Petra had never seen her father cry. She remembered the stories about the times he had cried, but she had never seen it or heard it. The sound of it tore at her heart. She settled the children and tried to eat breakfast.

These were times when she wanted the world to stop so that she could feel her way slowly through the pain, but the world would not stop. The cotton still needed to be picked, the dishes still needed to be washed, and children still needed to be mothered.

After breakfast, she left Josefa to clean up, and she grabbed her bonnet and hurried out with Austacio, Ignacio, and Plutarco to pick the cotton. Jesus rode off to make arrangements for burial. Friends and family came and went throughout the day, but Petra stayed in the field.

Cotton-picking gave Petra time to be alone with her thoughts. Today her thoughts were of her abuelita, her sweet, loving abuelita. *Keeper of the stories.* The words echoed in her head. She would always remember the stories and tell them again and again. That day as she worked, she told the story back to herself again, remembering each detail.

Cotton-picking stopped the next day so that the family could bury Clara. Again Reverend Elias shared words of comfort and prayed with her family in their time of grief. Clara was greatly missed. In the months that followed, as a tribute to her abuelita, Petra captured memories and added them to the family story.

Chapter 22
July 1886

Petra went out into the field thinking of her abuelita. A year had passed so quickly. The day in the field started out as usual, but about mid-day Petra looked up from her cotton-picking to see a tall Englishman watching her as he walked near the horse trough. He smiled when she looked his way. She returned his smile and resumed her work, curious about who he was.

The rest of that afternoon, as she pulled cotton from its boll and loaded her bag, she wondered about the Englishman. Later that day, she learned from her brother, Ignacio, that the Englishman was hired by the landowner to come around and water the horses.

The next day she saw the Englishman in the field again. He waved, and she smiled back. Several days passed in the same way. Then late one afternoon, the Englishman walked up to her in the field and handed her flowers.

Before she could speak, he tipped his hat and walked away. Petra called out a "Thank you" to the stranger and inhaled the sweet fragrance of the wildflowers. She carefully tucked the flowers in a pocket and went back to work filling her bag of cotton.

When her cotton sack was safely in the barn, she ran inside and put the flowers in water. She sat the mug full of flowers on her bedside table. That night she gazed at her flowers in the moonlight as she lay in bed and prayed. She prayed a special prayer for the Englishman and wondered when she would see him again.

A few weeks later when Petra was tending to the garden, the Englishman walked over to her after watering the horses.

"I'll give you my heart in exchange for yours," he said smiling and pointing from his heart to hers.

"I do not even know your name," Petra answered, surprised.

"Jasper. Jasper Suttles. Now will you marry me?"

"Come back tomorrow, and I will give you my answer."

Jasper bowed a gentleman's bow and promised to return tomorrow.

That night Petra prayed, asking God for guidance in her decision. How can I love again? How can I feel something for someone I just met? But I do feel something. Her thoughts became prayers, and soon she drifted off to sleep, sure of her answer.

※

Jasper was at her house just after daybreak. As the family was sitting down to breakfast, there was a knock at the door. Petra opened the door and almost jumped. She had not expected him so early.

"Good Morning! You said to come tomorrow. It is tomorrow. I am here." Jasper stood holding his hat as he spoke.

"Come in and join us. We are eating breakfast," Petra said as she stepped aside to let him enter.

She answered the questioning looks at the table with two simple statements. "This is Jasper Suttles. He proposed to me, and I accepted."

She wasn't sure who gasped and who cheered, but everyone could see that Jasper was happy with her answer.

Jasper looked over to Jesus and asked, "Will you give us your blessing, Sir?"

Jesus nodded.

Chapter 23
October 1886

Petra woke early and laid out her dress. She fingered the lace and felt her heart pounding. Her mamá quietly slipped into the room and handed Petra a small bundle. "I should have given this to you long ago. It belongs to you now."

Petra unwrapped the bundle and stared at the blue rebozo. "But, Mamá," she protested, "I cannot accept this."

Jesusa smiled. "It is your turn, Petra. The blue rebozo belongs to you, now."

That day, in her cream-colored dress and blue rebozo, Petra married Jasper Suttles. Reverend Elias Robertson performed the ceremony, and her parents stood as witnesses. After the wedding, the family gathered at Jesusa's cabin and enjoyed a celebratory meal. Everyone ate until they were full, then the ladies quickly straightened the kitchen. Once the bustle of chores was complete, Petra quieted the group. She held Jasper's hand and said, "My Jasper has not heard our story. I think I should tell him our story."

Everyone agreed. A few tears were shed. The story had not been told since Clara's passing. Petra draped the blue rebozo around her shoulders and held little Elias in her lap.

* * * * * * * * * * * * * * *

A long time ago before you were born, or your Mamá was born, or your abuela was born, even before your abuelita was born, when our family still lived near the big hacienda at the edge of the mountains, there was a girl – Leonor. Leonor was beautiful. Her long, black hair swayed gracefully as she walked and they say her eyes were so beautiful that you could see into her heart when you gazed into them. But in her village, El Potosi, there was no man for Leonor.

* * * * * * * * * * * * * * *

Petra recounted the story, skimming some parts and elaborating on others. She finished the story with the most recent happenings.

* * * * * * * * * * * * * * *

After Francisco died, I was not sure that love would find me again, but one day in the field, an Englishman smiled at me from afar. He brought me flowers and offered me his heart in exchange for mine. Love blossomed anew.

* * * * * * * * * * * * * * *

"Today we married, and the story continues," Petra said.

Chapter 24
July 1899

Petra stood on the porch watching the wagon loaded with trunks pull away. Tears persisted even as she wiped them away. She turned from the porch and walked inside the empty cabin. She'd lived here with her family before she married, again after the death of Mr. Torres, and yet again after Francisco's passing. These last several years, she'd lived only a short walk away. Soon after the wedding, when a sharecropper cabin had become available, Jasper became a sharecropper for the same landowner. She walked back out and sat on the porch steps. She thought of all the nights that she'd spent crying on the porch or leaning against Francisco. There were so many memories in the cabin. She could almost see her abuelita, Clara, in the rocking chair.

Jasper had run to this cabin to deliver the news to her mamá when Jasper, Jr. was ready to make his grand appearance in this world. She and Jasper had just celebrated their first anniversary. The family all gathered in this cabin to meet the new baby boy.

She remembered the night, long ago, after a family gathering when she and Jasper were walking home from the cabin. She told him that she was expecting again. He'd pulled her close and kissed her.

"I hope we have a girl, a girl that looks just like her mamá." She remembered him saying.

The little girl born months later did look like her mamá. Jasper named her Maria, as a tribute to the sister she never got to meet.

Petra wiped away a few more tears.

After Maria, Emma was born. Sweet Emma. And then Edward. Petra could almost see them running around the porch as they so often did when visiting their abuela's cabin.

Then she remembered the afternoon, only weeks ago, when her sister, Josefa, ran to Petra calling frantically for help. "Papá collapsed!" They found him on this porch, alive, but not well. They carried him to the bed, all of them working together. He struggled to breathe, and his pain was obvious. He'd asked to speak with Jesusa alone. Petra left the room so that her parents could talk, but stood right outside the door so that she could hear what was said.

Jesusa stood by the bed holding Jesus's hand. Petra would never forget what he said. "Jesusa, where I am going, you cannot go. I must make this journey alone." He pulled her hand to his lips and kissed it. "I love you, Jesusa."

"Jesus, I will follow you anywhere, and one day I will see you again. I love you, too," Jesusa replied as she sobbed silently and pulled his hand to her heart.

When the doctor arrived, Jesusa told him that Jesus no longer needed a doctor.

The days that followed were the hardest for the family since Francisco's passing. Jesusa and Josefa packed up their belongings and made preparations to move in with Petra's older brother, Jesus.

"Mamá, you and Josefa can live with us." Petra offered again and again.

"No, I cannot stay here. My boys are married and have their own families. You need to tend to your family, Petra. Thank you for offering, but we are going to live with your brother."

Now that the cabin was empty, Petra felt almost alone. She'd always had family near. As if reading her thoughts, Jasper walked up to the porch and sat down next to her.

Petra leaned her head against his shoulder. "My love, things have changed so much. I am thankful that God sent you to me."

Jasper wrapped his arm around her shoulders "I am, too."

Chapter 25
September 1899

Jasper arrived home whistling a tune.

"You are especially cheerful tonight," Petra commented as she served him a plate of food.

"Yes. Tomorrow we will take a ride so that you can see why I am cheerful."

Petra eyed him curiously, but Jasper just smiled.

The next morning Jasper hitched the horses to the wagon. Petra climbed up and sat next to him; Candida, Alcario, Francisco, Elias, Maria, Emma, Jasper Jr, and Edward all piled into the back of the wagon. For a while they bumped along quietly, occasionally commenting on the view before them. But then Jasper started telling them about where they were headed. He was taking them to an area called New Berlin, to a piece of land on Woman Hollering Creek.

Petra's memory flashed back to that day in the kitchen when she first heard the story. "Awful story. I cannot believe they named the creek that!"

"I know it is a horrid name, but it is beautiful land. After several great cotton harvests and years of hard work, we managed to save some money. I used a large portion of what we saved …" Jasper pulled the wagon to a stop and pointed. "I bought us that farm."

Tears gathered in Petra's eyes. The children clapped and cheered.

Jasper prodded the horses into motion and soon they were in front of the farmhouse. "Let's go in!" Jasper said as he climbed down and offered a hand to Petra.

It was far bigger than their cabin and had one more bedroom. The children wandered from room to room admiring the house. Jasper put his arms around Petra. "I hope you like it."

"I do like it. It is more than I ever expected to have. Oh how my life has changed. So many blessings."

The next two weeks were spent packing. They loaded trunks onto the wagon, and the family said goodbye to the little sharecropper cabin and moved to the farm.

Petra and Jasper lived on that farm and loved each other for many years. During the next nineteen years they watched their children grow, marry, and have children of their own. And many times during those years, Petra told her children and grandchildren her abuelita's story – the story of their family.

Epilogue
Feb 1918

When Jasper was slow to get out of bed, Petra knew he was ill. The Spanish flu was widespread in the area and claiming many causalities. Petra looked after Jasper day and night. Then she, too, came down with the Spanish Flu. When Candida learned they were both ill, she came to stay at the house and cared for them.

It was early in the morning. Candida was busy cleaning and preparing food when Petra called out to her. "Candida, come here."

"Yes, Mamá, what do you need?" Candida said as she walked into the bedroom.

"I want to talk to you." Petra said waving her toward the bed. Then she glanced over at Jasper who was sleeping peacefully.

Candida followed her gaze and quickly said, "He's better, Mamá. He's improving. Soon you will both be well."

Petra lowered her voice, "No, Mija. Go to the chest and open it. See the wrapped bundle?"

Candida opened the chest and found the bundle.

"Open it. It belongs to you now. I am sorry I waited so long to give it to you. The stories belong to you now. It is your turn."

"Oh, Mamá, the rebozo! I will always remember the stories, but you will be here to tell them to me and my children for many years. You will be well soon."

"No, Candida, the stories and the rebozo belong to you now. Heaven is calling me home." Petra shifted in her bed. She reached up and pulled the hair comb from her hair. "And this, so that you never forget."

Candida took the comb and held it gently in her hand. "Mamá, this is yours. When you are well, I will return it to you."

"Please leave me alone with Jasper, I want to talk with him. I love you, Candida. Always remember that."

Candida nodded, tears streaming down her face, and quietly walked toward the door.

"Oh, Candida, one more thing. When I die, please leave me in this bed until tomorrow morning."

"Mamá, you will be well, soon." Candida's heart ached hearing her mother's words.

"But you will do as I ask?"

"Yes, Mamá," Candida said through tears. Then she walked out of the room and closed the door.

Petra looked over at the bed next to her. "Jasper, are you awake?"

"Yes, Petra, I am awake. How are you feeling?"

"Not well. Today I will die, but I will come for you. Will you go with me?"

"Yes, my Petra, I would rather be with you anywhere than here without you." He reached his hand toward her, but saw her eyes close and knew that she was gone. He rolled over, crying into his pillow, praying that she would come for him.

※

The day was chaotic and tearful. Candida did as her mother asked and let her stay in her bed until the next morning. People were in and out of the room much of the day. In the evening things calmed down, and Jasper could hear the family gathered in the farmhouse.

Candida wrapped herself in the blue rebozo, wiped tears from her eyes, and began the story.

* * * * * * * * * * * * * * * *

A long time ago before you were born, or I was born or your grandma was born, even before your great grandma or great great grandma were born when our family still lived near the big hacienda at the edge of the mountains, there was a girl – Leonor. Leonor was beautiful.

* * * * * * * * * * * * * * *

Jasper smiled. He hoped that Petra could hear Candida telling the story. As he listened, he waited and prayed. Later that night, when the house was cloaked in stillness and silence, Jasper heard Petra calling to him. He smiled as he breathed his last and joined her in eternity that very night.

Facts, Dates, & Family History

* El Potosi is a village in the high plains near the southern end of the Sierra Madre Oriental Mountains in Nuevo Leon, Mexico.

* Leonor was christened in El Potosi on 22 May 1772. She was the daughter of Domingo Cortez and Maria de los Santos Barrientos.

* On Thursday, 4 Feb 1790, Esteban married Leonor. In the marriage entry, the priest noted that Esteban was from Ojo Caliente and that his parents were Vicente Gutierres and Bernarda de la Vega. He noted that Leonor was "india" (Indian or indigenous).

* Esteban and Leonor had at least 10 children: Dionicio (1795), Maria Josefa de Dolores (1797), Clara (1799), Hemeterio (1801), Jose Maria (1804), Jacinta (1806), Lucas (1808), Santos (1810), Manuel (1813), and Bruno (1815).

* Clara and Jose were married on Wednesday, 21 Jul 1819. They had 10 children: Jesus (1820), Casildo (1822), Paula (1824), Juliana (1825), Valentin (1827), Felipe (1830), Nicolaza (1833), Lucia (1835), Grabiela (1838), Agapita (1840).

* Jesus, age 28, married Maria de Jesus (Jesusa), age 18, on 18 Sep 1848. Her parents were Cayetano Perales and Gertrudis Rosas. They had 10 children and adopted one: Porfiria (1849), Maria de San Juan (1851), Jesus (1853), Petra (1856), Manuela (1860), Josefa (1862), Austacio (1864), Gregorio (1866), Ignacio (1868), Plutarco (1870), and Estefana.

* The death of Maria de San Juan at age 14 months is recorded in the Catholic records in El Potosi. She died of a fever.

* Gregorio's death is recorded in the Civil records in Saltillo. He also died of a fever.

* Information passed down through the family told of an adopted daughter. This was confirmed by marriage and death records. She was born Estefana Losano, but was adopted and raised by the Ramirez family. The story of how she was adopted is unknown.

* There is a recorded incident of an Indian attack in a place named El Peñuelo. Men from El Potosi did go and search for survivors.

* Jesus's siblings, Felipe and Agapita, and their families also moved to Saltillo sometime after Jesus and Jesusa moved.

* Jesusa's sister married a Cardona. The Cardonas also moved to Saltillo.

* Francisco and Lucio Guajardo were born in El Potosi. Their parents and siblings moved to Saltillo about the same time as Petra's family.

* Plutarco, the youngest son of Jesus and Jesusa was christened in Saltillo in 1870. The immigration date on later censuses is recorded as 1872.

* Petra married Mr. Torres on 13 Apr 1874. I was told by Petra's granddaughter-in-law that Petra was much younger than her first husband; her father signed permission on 25 Mar 1874 for her to marry.

* The story of Mr. Torres' death was recounted to me by a great grandson of Petra: A stranger asked Mr. Torres for a ride. The stranger seemed a little off, but Mr. Torres let him ride behind him on his horse. The stranger reached around, stabbed him in the abdomen, slid down off the horse, and ran off.

* There is an 1880 census record for the household of Jesus Ramirez. (Names are horribly misspelled in that census; I have listed them here with the correct spelling.) In the household were: Jesus (head of household), Jesusa (wife), Josefa (daughter), Austacio (son), Estefana (daughter), Petra (daughter & widow), Plutarco (son), Alcario (grandson), Samuel (grandson), Candida (granddaughter), Clara (mother), Lucio Guajardo (works on farm) and Francisco Guajardo (works on farm).

* The 1880 census notes that the house was rented, and they were working on a farm in a rural area outside the town of Seguin, Texas.

* Petra and Francisco were married by a Justice of the Peace on 29 Oct 1880 in Guadalupe County, Texas.

* Petra's children and their ages were gleaned from census records, birth records, and christening records. According to her christening record, Petra's and Francisco's daughter, Maria, was born in Mar 1881, but was not christened until Jan 1882.

* There is no record of the death of Samuel or Maria, but they are missing from later census records and family stories.

* Estefana and Lucio married in Feb 1881. Estefana was about 14 years old.

* There is no record of when or how Francisco died.

* Petra married Jasper Suttles in Oct 1886. Reverend Elias Robertson, a Methodist minister, performed the ceremony. Jesus and Jesusa stood as witnesses.

* The story of Jasper's proposal—my heart for your heart— was passed down through the family. However, Petra did not speak English at the time, and Jasper did not speak Spanish. He motioned as he said it because of the language barrier.

* The story of Petra's death and how she would come for Jasper was also passed down through the family. Dates on the death certificates indicate that Jasper died the day after Petra, both from the Spanish Flu. Many people in the family said that she died in the morning and he died in the middle of the night.

* Petra's brother, Jesus, was married to Urbana and living in Wilson county at the time of the 1880 census. He was listed as a shoemaker. His oldest daughter was named Leonor.

* The story about Jesus hiding in the pigsty was passed down through the family, as was the story of him wearing a dress to cross the border.

* "It Is Well With My Soul" was written by Horatio Spafford. It was first published in 1876.

* There is a creek named Woman Hollering Creek in east Bexar County, Texas, that runs toward New Berlin, Texas. Stories of how the creek got its name vary.

Family Trees

Leonor   **&**   Esteban

Dionicio

Josefa

Clara

Hemeterio

Jose Maria

Jacinta

Lucas

Santos

Manuel

Bruno

Clara & Jose

Jesus

Casildo

Paula

Juliana

Valentin

Felipe

Nicolaza

Lucia

Grabiela

Agapita

Jesus & Jesusa

Porfiria
Maria de San Juan
Jesus
Petra
Manuela
Josefa
Austacio
Gregorio
Ignacio
Plutarco
& Estefana Losano

Petra   &   Mr. Torres

Alcario

Samuel

Candida

Petra   &   Francisco

Maria

Francisco

Elias

Petra   &   Jasper

Jasper, Jr

Maria

Emma

Edward

About the Author

Pamela Humphrey has long been interested in researching her family history. After digging into her great grandmother's roots, she authored Researching Ramirez: On the Trail of the Jesus Ramirez Family. Pamela is an amateur genealogist and researcher of family stories. When she is not searching records for traces of the past, she might be writing, reading, crafting, or homeschooling. She lives in San Antonio, Texas, with her husband, sons, cats, leopard gecko, and beta fish.

You can connect with Pamela online:

www.phreypress.com

twitter.com/phreypress

facebook.com/phreypress